A
Harlequin
Romance

OTHER
Harlequin Romances
by JANE DONNELLY

1227—A MAN APART
1332—DON'T WALK ALONE
1376—SHADOWS FROM THE SEA
1432—TAKE THE FAR DREAM
1462—THE MAN IN THE NEXT ROOM
1483—NEVER TURN BACK
1548—HALFWAY TO THE STARS
1592—THE MILL IN THE MEADOW
1660—A STRANGER CAME
1681—THE LONG SHADOW

ROCKS UNDER SHINING WATER

by

JANE DONNELLY

HARLEQUIN BOOKS

TORONTO
WINNIPEG

Original hard cover edition published in 1973
by Mills & Boon Limited.

© Jane Donnelly 1973

SBN 373-01723-5

Harlequin edition published October 1973

Printed in Canada

CHAPTER ONE

TIMOTHY would wake soon. These days he always woke early. Jenny Douglas lay still and silent on the settee that was serving as a bed in her living-room. The clock said almost six, the door into the bedroom was slightly ajar, and soon the child sleeping in Jenny's bed would stir and whimper and unless he heard her moving around would quietly sob his heart out for his mother.

He was only seven years old, but he kept his tears for when he was alone. As Jenny did. If she had not had Timothy to consider the grief that welled in her now, choking in her throat, stinging behind closed eyelids, would have found relief in a storm of weeping.

Instead she held back the tears, as she did each morning when she woke and remembered . . .

. . . Two weeks ago the phone had rung downstairs and it had been Caterine. 'Jenny? Can I come over for a few days?'

'When?' Jenny had been buoyant with delight.

'Now.'

But it was mid-afternoon and the Cornish coast was a long way from this Midland town, and Caterine would be driving through the night.

Jenny had suggested, 'It might be better to start first thing in the morning,' but Caterine was positive that she needed a change of scene right now.

'There's another storm blowing up and that'll be the umpteenth this month, and I need to get away before I go spare on storms.'

'The weather's foul here too,' Jenny sighed. 'What a summer we've had!' It was a dreary day, rain was spattering on the coloured glass panel of the front door, and her sister laughed derisively.

'You don't know what foul weather is.'

Jenny laughed too, accepting there was no real comparison between inland storms when your home was pro-

5

tected by streets of buildings all acting as windbreaks, and the rage of elements around Caterine's house, high on the cliffs, overlooking the sea and the jagged rocks.

'So expect me with the dawn,' Caterine had said, putting down the receiver, and Jenny had rushed out to buy a bottle of wine and food to stock the fridge with flair, because Caterine was not the girl to dine on fish fingers, and the two lamb chops and half a pound of sausages that would have seen Jenny through the weekend.

'My sister's coming,' she had told Louie Sumner, who lived in the ground floor flat with her husband.

Louie didn't know Caterine. The Sumners had only lived here four months. But she had seen the photographs and she'd said, 'Nice! Shall we get to meet her?'

'Of course.'

And you'll both be bowled over, Jenny had thought as she staggered upstairs, arms around the huge carrier bag of foodstuffs. You won't believe such a spellbinder can be my sister. Except for the nose – we do have the same nose.

She apologized in advance, 'Heaven knows what time she'll get here, she's driving through the night. She is an idiot, but that's Caterine, everything's got to be now. I'll get down as fast as I can when she starts banging on the door. I hope she won't wake you.'

'Not to bother,' Louie said cheerfully.

When the phone rang again some hours later Louie had answered it and carolled up, 'Jenny!'

Jenny didn't get many calls, although it was legally her telephone. She'd wondered, 'Who is it?' as she'd hurried down, and Louie had shrugged and grinned.

'He wasn't saying.'

It was Caterine's husband, Paul Tremain. He had a deep voice. He was a big man, with dark hair and solid build. Jenny never felt really relaxed on the rare occasions when she met him, but tonight the moment he said his name she was terrified. She knew he was going to tell her, 'There's been an accident.'

She said, 'No . . .' shrilly as though denial could change it. 'Oh God – no!' then, whispering, 'How bad?'

6

Paul asked, 'Is the girl who answered the phone still there?'

'Yes.' If she had been alone would he have proceeded more gently, coming to it in circuitous fashion? Jenny's muted scream had halted Louie in her doorway. She stood now, pale, staring at Jenny, and Paul said huskily,

'Caterine's dead.'

Jenny crumpled. Her mind reacted so violently that it was like an explosion in her head. She dropped the receiver and it swung gently to and fro on its spiral wire. She covered her face with her hands, her short dark hair falling forward, then felt Louie's arms around her and heard Louie saying, 'Come and sit down, come on, Jen.'

In their living-room Bryan Sumner had the table covered with papers brought home from his work. He jumped up as Louie steered Jenny into the room and told him shakily, 'Jenny's just had some bad news, Bry. There's someone still on the phone.'

Bryan went out into the hall, closing the door after him. Louie was almost sure what the news was. Jenny had no one but her sister who was driving up here tonight, and she had the stricken look of a girl told the worst that could happen.

Jenny said, 'Caterine's dead.'

Louie had never met Caterine, but this was the house where Caterine had been born and there were the photographs of her and she had been on her way here tonight. It was nothing like the death of a stranger. Louie felt sick with shock and pity for Jenny. She said, 'I'll get you a drink.'

Jenny hardly heard, although she shook her head. She was numbed, frozen, she could never believe it. It was impossible to believe in a world without Caterine. Caterine was the shining one for whom the good things always happened. She had so much talent, all the gifts. Loveliness and love, a rich husband who adored her, Timothy ...

Timothy. .... Jenny ran back into the hall, snatching the phone out of Bryan Summer's hand. 'Paul?'

'Yes, Jenny?' said Paul.

'Timothy wasn't with her?'

'No,' he said quickly, and she handed the phone back to Bryan as though it had been his call she had interrupted. Caterine almost always brought Timothy. That was something to thank God for as soon as Jenny could feel anything again.

Louie made her drink hot sweet tea, and when Bryan came into the room he said, 'God, what a terrible thing! Jenny, you know if there's anything we can do.'

'Thank you,' she said. 'I'm glad you were here.'

To have taken that news alone would have been unbearable, even worse if it had happened six months ago when their mother was alive. Mrs. Douglas had been an invalid for a long time, but if she had been strong and hale the news of Caterine's death would have felled her. Caterine was her joy, her favourite. Caterine was everyone's favourite, and Jenny hadn't resented it because she loved Caterine too.

She asked Bryan, 'What did Paul tell you?'

He was wondering how much more she could take. She was a nice girl, quiet and pretty. She had always seemed sensible and calm, but he had never seen her in shock before. He didn't want to add to her distress by going into vivid detail until she was over the first blow. He said, 'The car skidded.'

'Where did it happen?'

'Not far from the house.' All the roads were hazardous. Those leading down to the coves were no more than tracks. The only road into the little harbour of Tremain was steep and cobbled and ran like a mountain torrent when there were storms.

But Caterine would be taking the main road along the top of the cliffs. A storm was coming, she'd said when she spoke to Jenny. Another storm.

Jenny saw the house, recalling as clearly as though she stood at an upper window: the main entrance faced the inland approach, there was a wide lawn edged with laurel and cedars and a thick yew hedge, and a drive that opened on to the cliff top road. Caterine would have turned right in her lime-green sports car, and skidded not far from the house.

Jenny asked dully, 'What happened?' She could see the car, going over the cliff's edge, falling. When the sea was up the razor rocks below were hidden except for plumes of spray. When there was a storm the white-tipped waves reached like hands. It was a long way down.

Bryan gulped and Jenny's voice raised. 'She went off the road? She went over the cliff?' He nodded, looking sick himself. Her brother-in-law to whom he had just spoken had said, 'If you could tell Jenny how it happened before she reads it in the newspapers I'd appreciate that, and would you take care of her tonight?'

Jenny said stupidly, 'She should have waited till tomorrow. Paul shouldn't have let her come if the storm had started and the roads weren't safe.' Then she bit her lip. 'I want to blame someone. Of course he thought it was safe. I just want to scream at someone.'

But there was no relief and no redress. Everything seemed so normal, as if nothing had happened. Upstairs her fridge was full of the food she had stacked away as she planned what they would do next week, she and Caterine and probably Timothy. Her family. Caterine, who looked like a young girl and would never grow old now, and whom Jenny would never see again.

Jenny sat hunched, hugging herself in her own arms, asking herself, 'What am I going to do?'

'You'll stay here with us tonight,' said Louie gently.

Bryan agreed. He had assured the man on the phone that Jenny wouldn't be left alone, but he felt that for a while he should leave her to Louie. Louie half pointed at the papers on the table and Bryan gathered them together and took them into the bedroom, where he had a desk and where he sometimes worked.

He was supposed to have this lot in order by Monday morning, but he wouldn't. He kept thinking of Jenny, and of the man who had just been explaining how his wife had died. Paul Tremain had sounded like an automaton, speaking with terse lucidity. Bryan couldn't have done that if anything had happened to Louie, he would have gone to pieces. But he had no doubt at all that Paul Tremain's self-control had covered a terrible grief.

Louie Sumner had grown fond of Jenny in the four months they had lived under Jenny's roof. After her mother had died Jenny had let off part of the house: the whole of the downstairs to Louie and Bryan, two rooms upstairs to a retired couple who were away this week-end.

It had been a godsend for Louie and Bryan, not long married and living on sufferance with his parents and two brothers, to find a furnished flat at a rent that wasn't out to grab the last penny. They were the first to apply and they took it on sight, waiting for the hidden snags to develop. When no snags did they blessed their stars and decided that the seemingly nice girl who owned the house really was a nice girl and honest in her dealings.

Jenny had been satisfied with her bargain. The old age pensioners upstairs were homely and kind, and Louie Sumner was bright and about Jenny's own age.

Jenny didn't have many friends of her own age. Her father had died the year of Caterine's marriage, and her mother had been an invalid almost that long. In the last three years Mrs. Douglas had rarely left her room, and Jenny had finally had to give up the secretarial work in a lawyer's office that had earned her an independent living. She had eked a pittance from home typing and there had been her mother's small pension, and Paul Tremain had made them an allowance.

Jenny had never enjoyed feeling like the poor relation, the hanger-on, but as Caterine said it was her money as much as Paul's, he had promised her all his worldly goods. Caterine had laughed and Mrs. Douglas had said it was sweet of Paul. It had kept Mrs. Douglas in comfort. There had been talk of getting a nurse in, but that would have cost more than Jenny doing the nursing, and her mother preferred having Jenny around.

Jenny couldn't regret that she had done all she could. She had loved her mother, although Mrs. Douglas had been a demanding and often querulous invalid, and at twenty-two Jenny was unlikely to step into the kind of job she might have had if she had stayed the course as a working girl.

She stopped accepting the allowance right away after her mother's death, although Caterine said that was stupid. Of course it wasn't charity and of course they could afford it. But under their father's will the small suburban house was now Jenny's – he had known Caterine would never need it, seeing the number of houses Paul Tremain owned – and Jenny planned to let, and she planned to work.

She had gone to an agency, and during the last four months had done holiday relief for four different firms while she strove for confidence and competence. She was out of practice on both.

The phone rang again and Bryan went quickly through the living-room. 'I'll get it.'

Jenny stopped breathing. Perhaps it was Paul again to say there had been a mistake, the car wasn't Caterine's. Or there had been a miracle and someone had noticed a flicker of heartbeat, and it was stronger now and Caterine had come to life again.

Bryan came back and said, 'Jack Wilson,' very quietly, apologizing that someone should be calling him on that phone at a time like this. Jenny thought – I should have spoken to Paul. If the car went into the sea how do they know for sure yet? She could have been thrown clear and lying above the water's reach. How do they know?

But she knew. She had a terrifying vision of Caterine, whole and happy one moment and the next plunged into a nightmare of whirling pain and choking darkness. Caterine, who had never been afraid or alone in her life.

The room began to disintegrate and she closed her eyes; Louie said softly, 'Don't faint, Jen. Put your head down.'

Jenny managed to open her eyes. 'I'm all right.'

Louie's own eyes were swimming with tears. Her voice was husky as she sat down on the small settee beside Jenny. 'You were very close, weren't you?'

Jenny nodded.

'Do you want to talk?' Talking wouldn't bring Caterine back, but Louie was desperately trying to break through Jenny's frozen whiteness. Jenny shook her head, and Louie was the one who wept.

Jenny stayed with Louie that night. She took sleeping pills and slept little, and by the next day the neighbours had heard. Some of them remembered Caterine living here, although she had left home for drama school at eighteen, and only came back for holidays. Then at twenty-one she had married Paul Tremain and joyously thrown up her promising career for love.

Jenny had been the only one with misgivings about that. She had been a schoolgirl and adored her talented sister, and when Caterine had told them before the wedding, 'Paul doesn't want me to be an actress, he just wants me to be a wife,' Jenny had thought he was asking a lot. He had been more than generous, Caterine had always had everything she wanted, but Jenny retained a little resentment that he invariably made Caterine turn down the offers of small parts that still sometimes came her way.

Several people had thought Caterine Douglas had the makings of stardom. But Paul was obdurate, and Caterine didn't seem to mind. She had talked about it with Jenny the last time they were together, after Mrs. Douglas died. 'It's flattering really, Paul's possessiveness. I wouldn't change him for any man I've ever met, he'd give me the moon if I asked for it. But,' she had smiled as though she didn't really mind this either, 'he's the master around Tremain, he makes the rules.'

The estate was his, but Jenny did not feel that should give him the ruling of flesh and blood too. She had never said so. It was Caterine's business and Caterine had always been happy, so had Timothy, their small son.

In the early years of the marriage Jenny and Mrs. Douglas had gone on holidays to the big house in Cornwall, but not after Mrs. Douglas became a confirmed invalid. After that Caterine would come here to see them, usually bringing Timothy with her.

Caterine's had been a wonderful life. Caterine had had

everything to live for, and the neighbours kept saying so. It didn't make it easier for Jenny. All Sunday folk with nothing but pity in their hearts filled the small house. They wanted to sympathize, they wanted to help, and they sat with Jenny and talked about Caterine, and Sunday was a dreadful day.

The Monday newspapers ran the story. Paul Tremain was a rich man. Besides the house, Moidores, he owned farms, a flourishing tin mine, and the village of Tremain. And Caterine was young and beautiful and had been an actress. Any car skidding from a cliff top would have been reported, but pictures of the Tremains were easy to come by, and the big house made an impressive shot. And the cliffs with the rocks below.

It was because of the pictures of the cliffs that her friends tried to keep the newspapers from Jenny, although she had seen the rocks and remembered them and carried them in her mind's eye from morning till night.

The verdict was 'Accidental death'. The skid marks were plain. It was weather in which extreme caution should have been taken, and Mrs. Tremain, happily off on a visit to her sister, had possibly not given her entire attention to the road surface.

Jenny did not have to attend the inquest; it would have been a grim ordeal, she was thankful to be spared it. Neither did she attend the funeral, but that was because Paul phoned again and asked her if Timothy could come up to her for a few days.

By then the funeral would be over. The house and the village must be under a monstrous shadow now, and there would be heartbreak enough for Timothy when he returned to begin life without a mother.

Paul said, 'He's asking for you.'

He would know where Caterine was going. She would have told him, 'I'm going to see Auntie Jen, only a little holiday. I'll bring you lovely presents back and you'll be good, won't you, and I'll phone you tomorrow.'

Perhaps he had a wild childish hope that if he spoke to Jenny she would say, 'Your mother's with me. Of course she's safe. They've all made a mistake.' Everyone hoped

13

that. Jenny had hoped, and she asked, 'How will he come?'

'Rolf Perrie will bring him.'

Rolf Perrie was manager of the tin mine. Jenny had met him years ago when she had gone on summer holidays. He had been a grave, rather gangling young engineering student, living with his parents on one of the smallholdings. She said, 'Yes,' and asked, 'How are you, Paul?'

'I'm all right,' said Paul Tremain. 'You?'

'I will be. Why did it happen?'

He said, 'I shouldn't have let her go. I should have stopped her.'

'Don't torture yourself,' she wanted to say, but even now she couldn't speak easily with him. He was too strong a man, too distant and powerful. She said, 'No one could help it.'

'No,' he said. 'Thank you for taking Timothy.'

She said, 'Thank you for sending him. He's all the family I have now.' She put down the phone because she couldn't say any more, a tight band was around her throat.

Timothy arrived late at night. Jenny opened the door when she heard the car draw up and the man who stood there was Rolf Perrie. He had always been slow to smile, and now the long drive and the heartbreak of his mission made him look years older than his age, but she recognized him and he said, 'Miss Douglas.'

'Where's Timothy?'

'In the car. He's asleep.'

The car was an estate model and she hurried out. Timothy lay curled in the back on a pile of cushions, covered by a red tartan rug. She knelt on the front seat and leaned over, feeling a rush of tenderness that made her want to reach for the child and hold him tight.

He was in deep slumber. By the light of the street lamp she saw his dark hair plastered to his damp forehead and his face shorn of all defence. He had always been a tough little boy, cheerfully belligerent, sparkling with mischief. But now he lay vulnerable and pitiful.

'I'll carry him in,' said Rolf Perrie. 'He's not been sleeping. You can understand that. As we came along he just went out like a light, and I tucked him up in the back.'

He opened the doors of the back of the car, and Jenny leaned over to put her fingers round Timothy's. He opened his eyes sleepily, seeing her through a haze. Then he grinned a little. 'Hello, Mom,' he said.

He thought she was Caterine. He wasn't awake yet, the light was dim, and there was that faint likeness between them. Then he blinked and saw her clearer and said, 'Auntie Jen.'

'Timmy.' She mustn't cry. She tried to smile and her lips quivered, and he wriggled himself up and turned and scrambled out of the van, past Rolf Perrie. He was reeling with sleep, but he had remembered. He came round the van to Jenny, and she held out her arms and he stumbled into them.

They clung together. Her cheek was wet against the child's cheek, and he said suddenly, 'Don't cry, Auntie Jen,' although they were his tears.

'No,' she promised. 'No.'

He took her hand and looked up at her. He had always looked like Caterine, with her gaiety and her bright charm, but now for the first time Jenny saw his father's face and thought – he will grow like Paul.

They went into the house and up to her room. She had a meal ready. She had arranged for Rolf Perrie to stay the night on a camp bed in the Sumners' flat before making the journey back to Tremain in the morning, but she had the meal here for the three of them.

She had hardly eaten herself for days, and Timothy simply pushed his food around. Rolf probably ate for courtesy's sake, he seemed to have no appetite either.

She remembered his home was a long grey stone building. There were horses that Jenny and Lorraine Tremain, Paul's young sister, used to ride. Lorraine rode very well, Jenny had only been on horseback on those holidays and she was not a natural rider. Once she had slithered off when a horse moved suddenly and they had taken her into the farmhouse to have a glass of fresh warm milk and get her breath back.

She reminded Rolf, 'Do you remember when I slid off a horse right into one of the pigsties?' This was really for Timothy, to coax a smile from him, and he grinned for her, but there wasn't much talking done.

Timothy looked tired, and when it was plain that no one was eating any more and Jenny said, 'It's very late, Tim, it's bedtime now,' he raised no objections.

He squirmed into bed yawning and she was almost sure he would fall asleep soon. He said, 'Good night, Auntie Jen,' and then, 'You don't get real storms here, do you?'

That was almost the last thing Caterine had said to Jenny. Jenny said gently, 'Not really. Good night, Timmy.'

Rolf Perrie was still in the living-room, sitting in the armchair, his head sunk low. When Jenny came out of the bedroom, closing the door, he said quietly, 'Settled down, has he?'

'I think he'll sleep. He's worn out.'

Rolf shook his head. 'Dreadful business. Dreadful.' He couldn't believe it either. He sounded bewildered, 'Mrs. Tremain, the last person you can think of as—' he couldn't say 'dead' to her sister. He said, 'She was always so alive.'

Caterine had enjoyed everything so much. It was a drab world for most, and tragic that someone who loved living should be extinguished.

There had been a photograph of Caterine on the sideboard; Jenny had moved it before Timothy came. She looked for it now without thinking, and saw it in her mind, Caterine laughing.

'Best for the lad to be out of Moidores for a while,' said Rolf. 'It's a dark house these days.' This house was dark too, thought Jenny, but at least there was human bustle and busyness outside, not the terrible loneliness of cliffs and seas and seagulls screaming.

Rolf Perrie cleared his throat and glanced at the closed bedroom door, then spoke in hardly more than a hoarse whisper. 'Timmy, you see – he saw it.'

'Saw *what*?'

'She said goodbye to them and went off in her car, and he ran upstairs to watch the car from one of the turret windows as far as he could.' Jenny had only imagined the road and the rain, and the little car skidding wildly and falling, turning, but the child had seen it.

Rolf Perrie said raggedly, deeply moved, 'He came screaming to the top of the stairs.'

'Oh *no*!' Jenny's heart clenched. How could they ever hope to wipe out that memory from a child's mind?

'A storm broke just afterwards,' said Rolf, 'and storms terrify him now. That's one of the reasons Paul wanted to get him out of Tremain for a few days.'

'I'll take care of him,' she promised, and wished she could promise to keep the storms away.

She made up her bed that night on the settee and then in the darkness she opened the door into the bedroom and listened to Timmy's steady breathing. He was peaceful yet, without dreams or nightmares. The nightmares would come with waking and she must be ready. She left the door a little ajar and slept the listening sleep of a mother with an ailing child.

She was awake first next morning, moving quietly around getting the breakfast when he stirred. She heard him stifling sobs and then he came out. He was not weeping, although his face was smeared. He didn't look as he had done while he slept, but as he had looked last night telling her not to cry, holding his lips steady, not with the wide gaze of a child but with the guarded eyes of a man.

Timothy helped Jenny through the next week at least as much as she helped him. There were no scenes and no tears, but they both knew that the other suffered and they both mourned.

Jenny filled the time. They shopped, they cooked meals and ate them. They took bus rides out of town, often to places they had visited with Caterine. She couldn't always avoid that, and sometimes Timothy would say, 'Mom liked it here, didn't she?' as though they were sharing with Caterine still.

On other holidays he had always been chattering, running ahead, eager for any action going. But now he was quieter and often now he reached for Jenny's hand.

She was going to miss him terribly when his father fetched him home. Work and friends weren't going to fill the void. Paul Tremain phoned each evening, always at the same time, and Timothy would tell him what they had been doing, but even Timothy went a little in awe of his father.

When Paul handed the phone over to Lorraine or to Ebby the housekeeper Timothy's tone of voice changed. He loved them all, and they loved him, but he was more at ease with the womenfolk.

Jenny understood that. She often spoke to Paul briefly before Timothy took his call. He couldn't have been more courteous, but she always felt that Paul Tremain's usual reaction to any sort of obtuseness would be irascibility. She always half expected to make a fool of herself. . . .

Tomorrow Timothy was leaving her, and when she woke this morning and remembered that Paul was coming today she couldn't hold back a sigh. She dreaded the moment of parting. It was going to be like losing her own child. If Timothy made any sort of fuss at all – she hoped and prayed he wouldn't, but after the phone call last night fixing the time of his father's arrival he had clung to Jenny like a limpet – if he did make a fuss Paul might be impatient with him and that would be heart-rending for Jenny.

She put on her housecoat and went into her tiny kitch-enette, and as she began to cook bacon she heard Timothy padding over the living-room lino. 'Hungry, Timmy?' she asked.

'No.' He had eaten better these last three days. She had done a lot of planning to tempt him to eat without him realizing it was strategy.

She said, 'I think I'm hungry.'

He stood in the doorway, scowling, looking so troubled that she longed to comfort him. 'I don't want to go back,' he gulped. 'I want to stay with you.'

She wanted that too. She had to keep the wistfulness out of her voice and speak lightly. 'What about your father, and Lorraine? Whatever would they do?'

He was torn between loyalties and Jenny said, 'You must go home, Tim, they couldn't manage without you, but you can always come for holidays, and I'll come and see you.'

He watched her warily. 'You wouldn't be scared?'

'Scared?' she echoed.

'When the storms came.' There was fear in his voice and in his small tense face. 'Of the sea witch.'

That old story. The legend Jenny had thought so romantic when she first heard it, at fifteen on her first holiday at Tremain, of an ancestor of the Tremains who fell in love with a sea witch and tried to keep her on land. But she escaped back to the sea and sometimes when the storms came sang her siren song that could lure anyone who heard it.

'Sea witch weather,' they called the wildest storms along the coastline of Tremain, and the tiny island, inhabited by birds, that could be seen on the skyline from the harbour was the Witch's Rock. It was part of local folk lore, like the wrecker tales. Timothy had never feared the sea witch before.

But that was before the sea took Caterine. In a child's mind something could have reached for that car.

Jenny decided that she must phone Lorraine and tell her. It was years since she had met Paul's sister, but Lorraine was only a few months older than Jenny and the two girls had been holiday companions years ago. Lorraine had been thrilled then with her dazzling new sister-in-law, adoring Caterine on sight, and she had stayed devoted to Caterine. Caterine's death must have been traumatic for her, and Lorraine was a delicate girl. In the long run Lorraine could be more affected than Jenny, who was physically stronger.

Lorraine would be mothering Timothy now. And Mrs. Ebsworth, 'Ebby', the housekeeper. They would take good care of Timothy.

Jenny said gently, 'The accident was because the car skidded. It could have happened anywhere, it was nothing to do with the sea. And the sea witch is only a fairy tale. You don't believe in fairy tales, do you?'

'*No.*' He was emphatic on that. 'Not in fairy tales,' he added.

They went round the market that morning. The stalls were varied and there was plenty to keep Timothy entertained. They had lunch at the Lotus Bough, because Chinese food was a change and going through the menu could be turned into a game.

Paul Tremain should have been arriving in the evening, that was what he had said. He had declined the offer of a night's lodging and said he would book into a hotel, come round in the evening and collect Timothy next morning.

Jenny had said, 'Just as you wish, of course,' relieved that he was going to a hotel.

After lunch they went to a film matinée and then back home. It was hardly tea-time, but outside the house there was a car that had to be Paul's. Jenny's heart sank as they turned the corner and she saw the car and Timothy said, 'Father's here.'

Louie came hurrying into the hall to tell them, 'Mr. Tremain's come. He went up.'

'Thank you,' said Jenny.

Timothy walked on, not hesitating but not hurrying, taking the stairs with deliberation, and Louie said very softly, 'I can see why the camp bed wouldn't have done for him.'

The camp bed had done very well for Rolf Perrie, who had been most appreciative, but one look at Paul Tremain had been enough to tell Louie that this man booked into the best hotel in town as a way of life.

She was sorry for him, of course, as sorry as she was for Jenny and Timothy. But after she had directed him to the rooms Jenny had kept for her own she realized she had let him go without offering a word of sympathy. Intrusion on his personal tragedy was beyond her.

Paul must have heard their footsteps in the passage. Before they reached the door he opened it and Timothy went quicker.

'Hello, Tim,' said Paul.

'Hello, Father.' Timothy looked very small hurrying towards the big man. Paul Tremain always had made things look small, Jenny remembered: rooms, people. He picked up Timothy and carried him into Jenny's living-room, and Timothy grinned, arms around his father's neck.

When he set down the child, who went running into the bedroom to fetch something to show him, he looked across at Jenny, a quick and searching look, checking for what?

He asked, 'How are you?' so it must have been concern, and she was touched by it.

'I'm well,' she said. She had seen Paul last at her mother's funeral. Before that not for some years, and not since. He didn't change. The lines in the strong-featured face were deep now, but she wondered – did you weep for Caterine?

She couldn't imagine him weeping. She felt that he would have shut himself away, and come back within a reasonable time, grief contained, to deal with the prob-lems that had to be dealt with. Even the problem of death.

Timothy had pictures from the zoo – they had been to Whipsnade on Wednesday – and Paul listened as Tim-othy explained and went into long accounts of what they had been doing and what they had seen.

Jenny watched Timothy, loving him, realizing at last that she should be offering Paul some sort of hospitality and apologizing, 'I'm sorry. Will you have some tea?'

'Not for me, thank you.'

She said, 'I'd better get ours.'

'I do the cooking. I get the tea,' said Timothy. 'Some-times.'

They had cheese on toast today and Timothy got it, and when it was eaten and cleared away Paul said, 'We have to make an early start in the morning, Tim, you'd better have an early night.'

Timothy pulled a face but went, dragging unwilling feet, to the bathroom, and when Jenny brought him back, pink and glowing, he kissed his father good night.

Jenny cuddled him and tucked him up as she did each night, and tonight he said, 'You will come, won't you?'

'Of course,' she promised.

'Soon?'

'As soon as I get a holiday.'

That seemed to satisfy him. At least he snuggled down between the sheets and she went back into the living-room. Paul signed to her to close the door. As she did he said, 'Thank you.'

'For having Timmy? I don't know how I'd have got through these days without him.'

He was sitting in the big chair. She sat at the table and wondered what it would be like eating here alone again.

'They haven't been easy days, have they?' said Paul.

'I still don't believe it.' There were still times when she didn't. He said:

'I wish I could say I didn't.' He would have seen Cater-ine, identified her, and Jenny asked quickly:

'How is everyone? How's Lorraine?'

'Taking it badly,' he said. 'She's been very near to a breakdown.' Lorraine had been shielded all her life, nothing like this could have happened to her before.

Paul said abruptly, 'Jenny, have you any immediate plans?'

'Plans?'

He put it another way. 'Is there any reason why you must stay here?'

'No.'

'Good. Then will you come down to Tremain for a month or so?'

She hadn't expected him to suggest that, but she said 'Yes' at once, without stopping for a moment to con-sider.

He looked relieved. She must be looking astonished be-cause it was a complete surprise. He said, 'Timothy is very fond of you, and I'm more than grateful for what you've done for him already.'

Timothy had been bright and nearer his normal self just now, but Jenny tried to explain, 'It wasn't all me.

22

Most of it was getting away from Tremain. When he gets back he could be afraid.'

'I know. But he has to come back and he has to feel secure again. If you could be around I think perhaps he might.'

She said, 'I'll try.' She would do more than try. She loved her sister's child with fierce protectiveness and she was so glad of this chance to be with him, to help him, not to lose him. She had been so afraid she was going to lose him.

She got up, trying to put this into words, and Paul said, 'Your time will be your own, of course, and I'll pay you what you'd be earning.'

'You will not!' There was no reason for her intensity of resentment, except that she felt like the poor relation again. She snapped, 'You're not employing me,' and was horrified at herself because that was downright rude and, worse, could mean that he would say, 'All right, forget it.'

She said, 'I'm sorry, but I don't want to be paid.'

'Of course I'm not employing you, but I am taking you away from your employment, and why should you be the loser?'

Put like that it was more unreasonable than ever, but she couldn't pick up a salary cheque for being with Timothy. She said, 'I'd rather not, if you don't mind, I do have some money coming in from the house.' She ventured a weak smile. 'And I presume I'd get board and lodging?'

'Then that's settled,' he said.

Jenny left with them next morning. She had packed after Paul left last night, and asked Louie to send on the mail and given her the phone number of Moidores. It had been that simple. No one was going to say, 'Don't go, Jenny,' because she had no really close friends. Caring for her mother all those years had kept her from making friends. She was a free agent now, rootless although she had lived in this house all her life – it was not the kind of house that put down roots.

She went out of the front door with Timothy skipping

by her side, and knew she wouldn't care if she never saw the place again. Although of course she would see it again. She was only going to Tremain for a little while, this was still her home.

Timothy was beaming. When she'd told him his delight had sent him leaping around like a crackerjack, and she had had a hard time steadying him before his father arrived. Paul wanted her to help Timothy back to a calm and stable way of life, not get him so over-excited that he was as near to tears as laughter.

But he calmed down when he heard the car – his father was a restraining influence – and jog-trotted out still talking about how smashing it was that Auntie Jen was coming.

It was a long drive, although the car went superbly. Paul didn't join in the conversation. In the back seat Jenny and Timothy chattered together, and read a book, and Jenny spun stories and made up games. Paul could have been a chauffeur or a taxi driver. Unless Timothy spoke to him he didn't speak, and then he would answer, mostly with information. Most of Timothy's remarks were along the lines of what's that? where are we? why is it? But everything Paul said had an economy that dealt with the subject and closed it.

They stopped for a meal, eating at a good restaurant that seemed to be crowded but where a table was quickly found for them; and as Jenny helped Timothy with his selection she met the appraising glances of two well-dressed women at the next table.

Maybe they were thinking she looked too young to be Timothy's mother – although Caterine had looked no older, only lovelier. Maybe they would decide she was the au pair girl; her clothes didn't match up to Paul's, which spoilt it as a family group.

Making weak jokes for herself helped to keep her spirits up. She was glad to be here with Timothy, but she was only here because Caterine was dead, and that thought was never out of her mind.

Paul must be thinking that too. Physically he was with them, but his thoughts were not. Jenny made no attempt

24

to draw him into conversation, she was here for Timothy and she confined herself to the child.

Timothy tired before the end of the journey and slept, huddled against Jenny, so that they drove for miles in silence, skirting the holiday resorts, coming on wilder lonelier country, where the roads were narrow and twisted, lined by high hedges through which every now and then they glimpsed the sea.

Jenny had not been to Tremain for years, but she remembered her first sight of it, and when it was signposted she looked for landmarks.

Tremain was a small natural harbour. For centuries fishing had been the livelihood of the men who lived in the little granite houses clustered around the quayside or clinging to the steep sides of the gorge. But now the tourist trade reached here in summer. There were shops, an artists' colony.

Rounding one spur of the coastline you could see the lights of Tremain in the gathering dusk, and on the cliffs just beyond, above another cove, you could see the house.

Moidores dominated the skyline. It was rather narrow and high. Early Victorian Tremains had renovated the central part and raised it. The wider, lower parts had been left; some converted to outbuildings, other parts crumbling away, their Tudor beams exposed to the elements.

Facing the cliff edge a row of trees had once been planted as protection against the winds from the sea. There were gaps where some had gone with the crumbling cliff, others slanted with parts of their roots showing over the edge.

It had always seemed to Jenny that this was the true face of the house, facing the sea. Not the house that faced the road, with its curved drive, smooth lawns and well cut hedges.

In the driver's seat Paul Tremain stayed silent, and they passed the little signpost pointing down to Tremain with the notice beneath 'No cars beyond this spot,' and drove on along the cliff road.

There must be clues to pinpoint the accident: a hedgerow smashed, a fence repaired. Jenny couldn't look, but as they went through the gates and down the drive she glanced up at the turret window through which Timothy must have watched the road.

The lights were on in a number of rooms, and Jenny said softly, 'Wake up, Timmy, we're home.'

He woke easily. Once he had needed shaking awake, but not now. He opened his eyes and blinked the drowsiness out of them and sat up.

The front door opened as the car stopped and the housekeeper, Mrs. Ebsworth, came out. She was a tall woman, rawboned, with iron grey hair drawn severely back and a smile of surprising sweetness. Timothy went running to her and she bent to kiss him, then straightened to smile at Jenny. 'My, it's a long time since we've seen you,' she said.

'You haven't changed a bit,' said Jenny. It wasn't that long, it was just something to say because Jenny was choked with emotion, and the grip of Ebby's hands told her the older woman was too.

They went into the hall, that hadn't changed, and the girl running down the stairs was Lorraine. She was as fair as her brother was dark, as fragile as he was strong. She was a very attractive girl and she and Jenny had been good friends in the old days.

Paul said, 'Jenny will be staying with us for a while.'

'Isn't that smashing?' said Timothy. Ebby nodded and smiled, agreeing. Lorraine stood at the bottom of the stairs looking at Jenny with a startled widening of the eyes. Then she came forward and put her arms around her and kissed her and said, 'Hello, Jenny, it's lovely to see you.'

But Lorraine's first reaction had not been welcome. Jenny was not sure what it had been.

CHAPTER TWO

'You should have told me,' Mrs. Ebsworth said severely. 'I'd have had a room ready.' She clicked her tongue at Paul and he said:

'The room next to Timothy's.'

So he hadn't left here intending to bring Jenny back with him. He must have made up his mind last night. She was a surprise to the women of the household, although now Lorraine was smiling tremulously.

Why didn't you want me here? Jenny wondered. Or did I imagine the way you just looked at me?

Mrs. Ebsworth said, 'There's a message from Mr. Morrison on your desk.'

'Thank you.' Paul turned towards the door that Jenny remembered as his office. 'Would you bring me some coffee and sandwiches in?'

He went into the office, and Mrs. Ebsworth began to tell Timothy that she had made some special gingerbread for him. If he came with her he could have a piece.

'Is Auntie Jen coming?' he wanted to know, and Jenny smiled and said she'd be along.

That seemed to do. He went, and none too soon because Lorraine's tears suddenly overflowed. She turned her face away. 'I'm sorry, Jenny,' she sobbed. 'I know you feel as badly as I do, and it's worse for Paul, but I can't help it.'

With her fragile physique and her translucent skin and the shadows like bruises around her eyes Jenny could believe that Lorraine's breaking point had been nearly reached. Lorraine had never been robust. On those holidays she had tired far sooner than Jenny, and now it was Jenny who did the comforting, so far as anyone could comfort.

Lorraine dried her tears, then went into the drawing-room and swallowed a couple of pills from a pretty little jewelled pill box on the mantelshelf. She said, 'The doctor gave me these. They do help.'

'Good,' said Jenny. For how long? she wondered. And how many was Lorraine taking? She had to go after Timothy, she had told him she was following and she must. But she could see why Paul had brought her here. Lorraine couldn't give Timothy a feeling of security again, Lorraine seemed lost herself.

Ebby was the solid one. Jenny remembered her with affection, and Alec Ebsworth her husband, 'Eb' the gardener. They were both in the kitchen with Timothy and they turned to look approvingly at Jenny, counting Timothy's impovement her doing.

'This is more like our lad,' said Eb.

Jenny's expression warned them the improvement could be temporary, and they knew it. But while Timothy ate his supper they pretended a mighty interest in everything he had done on his 'holiday' and when the child's chatter ran out on that subject Ebby asked, 'Where are you going to take Auntie Jenny tomorrow?'

'Down to the harbour first,' said Jenny. 'I want to see Tremain again.'

Lorraine came into the kitchen as Jenny was taking Timothy off for his bath. She was calm now, and she said, 'Bedtime, Timmy?'

'Yeah,' said Timothy wistfully.

'See you tomorrow,' said Lorraine. She ruffled his hair. 'I'm glad you're back, and I'm glad you brought Jenny.'

'She's having the room next to me.' Timothy looked up at Jenny. 'Not Mom's room. Nobody's ever going to have Mom's room, are they?'

'You must show me my room,' Jenny said quickly. 'I don't know which it is.'

'I'll show you,' said Timothy.

He had been a baby when Jenny was last here. In those days the nursery had had a frieze of flopsy bunnies and wall-eyed donkeys. Now it was a boy's room, three white walls, one navy; the nursery furniture exchanged for a sea chest, a bunk bed, fitted cupboards – one with a formica-topped working surface running the length of the wall under the windows.

There were posters of aeronauts and dinosaurs. Timothy seemed to be covering quite a range of evolution, and although the room was tidy now Jenny knew that with Timothy around again the cupboard doors would burst open, their contents spilling everywhere, and the desk top would be piled high.

A connecting door led into Jenny's room. The bed was made up and turned back, and it was a pleasant room.

With Timothy in bed Jenny unpacked, putting her clothes in the chest of drawers that smelt of lavender, or hanging them in the deep clothes closet. She took her time unpacking, and then she brushed her hair, watching herself in the oval Victorian mirror that swung on its stand on top of the chest of drawers.

She looked pale and felt she looked plain. This had been the nanny's room in the old days when families were larger. There was a schoolroom too. Lorraine had been privately educated. Not Paul. Charterhouse and Oxford, Paul.

I look like a Victorian governess, Jenny thought, pale and plain and meek. And she remembered Caterine with her tossing hair and glowing beauty and understood why their parents had loved Caterine best, why everyone loved Caterine best.

Timothy must have fallen asleep quickly. He was deep in slumber when she went to his bedside and looked down at him. She resisted the temptation to fuss, smoothing pillows or tucking in sheets, and went out of the room.

As she walked along the passage Lorraine called, 'Jenny!' A bedroom door was open and Lorraine sat on the dressing-table stool, turned to watch who passed the open door.

Jenny went in. They had giggled together as schoolgirls in here, but this room had changed as much as the nursery. The wall-to-wall carpeting was white and the walls shimmered with silk, the colour of a summer sky. Jenny asked, 'Whatever happened to the pop stars?'

Lorraine managed a smile. 'I grew out of them.' She looked around, as if she was trying to remember the way it used to be. 'Do you like it?'

'Who wouldn't? It's beautiful.'

'We had the rooms done about a couple of years ago.'

'The rooms?'

'This and Caterine's.'

Jenny remembered Caterine telling them about the top-name interior decorator who had redesigned some of the house. Caterine and Paul's bedroom had been in another wing, overlooking the sea.

Lorraine picked up a perfume bottle from the dressing-table, and dabbed pulse points lightly and nervously with a glass stopper. 'Caterine never did like the sound of the sea. She never got used to it, she couldn't sleep for it, so she had to have a room on this side of the house. She had the room right opposite the nursery.'

She put the scent down again and her eyes were dark and haunted. 'It's still Caterine's room, although everything's been put away and the bed's stripped down and Ebby's tried to make it look like an empty room.'

She gestured helplessly. 'Timothy keeps hiding in there, waiting for her, I suppose. Isn't that dreadful? The cupboards are full of her clothes and she chose the wall-paper and the curtains and the carpet, and it still *feels* like Caterine's room.'

'Now Timmy's back something will have to be done, won't it?' But Lorraine did not seem capable of doing anything, as she sat white-faced and stricken.

Locking the door or repapering the walls were short-term solutions, Jenny thought. Only time and love would get Timothy through this bewilderment of loss. He was very young and he was dearly loved, and he would come through it as Jenny herself must.

Lorraine said huskily, 'You weren't here, Jenny, you can't imagine how dreadful it was. I'll remember it all my life. When Timmy started screaming—'

Jenny didn't want to hear. She asked desperately, 'How's the shop going?'

Lorraine ran a crafts shop down by the harbour where most of the artists displayed their wares, but now she looked blank. 'The shop? Oh, the *shop*? I haven't been down since.'

She sounded as though the accident had stopped the world. She said, 'Someone's running it.'

Paul Tremain had someone running everything around here, this was his kingdom, but surely Lorraine would have been better in the shop than in the house, reliving the tragedy, taking tranquillizers.

Jenny's saving had been getting out with Timothy, and she said, 'Will you come down to the harbour with us in the morning?'

'I'll see how I feel.' Lorraine was not promising.

'Has it changed much?' asked Jenny.

'Tremain? No.'

'Still the same people?'

'There are some new faces among the artists, and some new men at the mine, but the families in Tremain are the same, and on the farms.' She gave Jenny a sidewards glance. 'Rolf Perrie brought Timmy up to you, didn't he?'

'Yes.' Something in Lorraine's voice made Jenny return the look with raised eyebrows.

Caterine had spoken of young men who were taken with Lorraine from time to time, but the affairs always seemed to peter out. Caterine would joke about them, 'If I don't watch it I'll have two spinster sisters.' She hadn't talked of Rolf Perrie and Jenny asked casually:

'Any particular man in your life right now?'

'No particular one.'

'Not Rolf?'

Lorraine was jerked out of her lassitude. 'Why on earth should you think that?'

'I don't really know,' Jenny admitted.

'Rolf Perrie? Heavens, *no!*' Perhaps it was because up to now her voice had been hushed and husky that this sounded so shrill that Jenny was left wondering.

Jenny was tired. She had a hot bath and got into bed, but was not surprised when she didn't fall asleep. She had brought up a book half expecting this, and stayed with it doggedly until her eyes began to blur and it was a relief to turn out the light.

You could hardly hear the sea at all in this room. Its sound was soothing and restful, and Jenny loved the sea. She remembered looking out from the other side of the house, thrilled by the magnificence of the view and Caterine beside her shuddering, saying, 'They used to lure the ships on to the rocks down there, and if one man or one animal got ashore alive it wasn't legally a wreck, so no one ever did.'

Caterine had not. Perhaps that was why she had always feared the sea. Jenny forced back the tears and made herself think of tomorrow while she waited for sleep. The time of weeping was over, life had to go on.

She woke to the faint rumble of thunder. It was some distance away, but it still sounded like storm, and storms terrified Timothy. She slipped out of bed and opened the dividing door between their rooms very quietly.

Moonlight shone on his bed, but there was no sign of Timothy, and Jenny ran out into the passage where light filtered opposite, edging the door of Caterine's room.

'Timmy goes in there, looking for Caterine,' Lorraine had said, and Jenny bit her lip, angry with herself. She should have woken sooner. She should never have let this happen.

She opened the door and called softly, 'Timmy,' and saw Paul. He stood by the window, the curtains were wide and the window showed only darkness. Her eyes were dazzled by the light, but as he came towards her she saw greyness through the tan of his skin as though he was a dying man. He asked curtly, 'What is it?'

'Timmy isn't in bed.'

He went past her across the corridor into the nursery. Through the open doors she saw him pull back the counterpane, then stoop to lift the child higher. Timothy had slithered down in sleep, under the sheets.

Paul said a few quiet words of reassurance, but Timothy didn't wake. Then he came back and Jenny said wretchedly, 'I should have looked closer, but I saw the light around the door and Lorraine told me he sometimes comes in here.'

'Yes.'

There were dustsheets on the furniture, but she could smell Caterine's perfume on the air. There was no other quite like it, floral but not sweet, a sharp scent that had been specially blended for her; persistent enough to make a child feel that the woman who always wore it was near. A child – or a man.

The cupboards were full of Caterine's clothes. To stir anything would be to stir fragrance.

Paul said, 'You'd better get back to bed.'

He closed the door after her and in her own room she picked up her watch and saw that it was past three o'clock. The night was almost over and Paul had been fully dressed, he couldn't have slept at all. And he had driven down from the Midlands yesterday and he was presumably working today. Grieving in that shrouded room could do nothing, except help to break him.

She turned slowly, reluctant, but unable to switch off the light and go to sleep. She tapped the door and he opened it and she said, 'Please don't stay here, please try to get some rest.'

He exclaimed, 'For God's sake!'

'I loved her too.' That was her only excuse. 'I know she wouldn't want—'

He said wearily, 'You don't know what you're talking about,' and shut the door in her face, but she had expected that. She went back to the child, the one she could help.

Timothy still slept, the thunder was still faint and far-away. She left the door ajar between her own room and the nursery, and lay awake until she was sure the storm was coming no nearer tonight.

Lorraine did not go down to the harbour with them. She said, 'Tomorrow, perhaps,' and Timothy tugged at Jenny's hand and urged,

'Come *on*, Auntie Jen.'

The sea always cut off the cove below Moidores from the harbour of Tremain. You reached Tremain either by rounding the cliffs by boat, or by the cliff top road, then down the cobbled way.

They had to pass where Caterine's car had crashed,

Jenny knew it by the tightening of Timothy's fingers round her hand. The road curved slightly here, but Caterine must have been travelling too fast to take her over the rough grasses and through the fencing. The prospect of a long journey ahead could have accounted for that, or simply that she was thinking of other things and misjudged.

Jenny talked all the way, about the people she used to know in Tremain. 'The pink house? Who lives in the pink house now, Timmy, the house on the corner by the quay?'

'Dan,' he said, 'and Mrs. Blaskie.'

'*Yes*,' said Jenny. 'He's a fisherman. Oh, I remember them. Start at the top of the hill and tell me all the way down.'

Timothy did, although before he had catalogued halfway down the hill they had reached the signpost and were passing the houses. There were no pavements, several of the houses clinging to the hillside did bed-and-breakfast and one was a guest house. There were shops, a pub called the Crow's Nest high on the hill, and another on the jetty called the Tremain Arms. At the bottom of the gorge narrow streets intersected, and around the little harbour were more houses, more shops.

It was picturesque and it was prosperous. Everything was brightly painted, some of the buildings colour-washed, some with white windows and doors contrasting with the grey of granite.

Today was a fine day, with visitors who had left their cars at the top walking down the steep and cobbled street, leaning over the harbour wall, spending their money and enjoying themselves.

All the locals knew Timothy, of course. They waved to him and called and looked to see who was with him. Even those who didn't remember Jenny saw her resemblance to Caterine and stopped smiling and looked sorry for her.

She bought ices from the sweet shop and Alice Pentreath, who had served behind this counter for twenty-five years, said, 'Hello, Jenny, it's nice to see you again,' and as Timothy skipped ahead out of the shop licking his

34

extra large cornet, 'I can't tell you how sorry everybody is. It's a wicked thing, she was a lovely girl.' Alice's round face went haggard, her gaze following Timothy. 'Poor little motherless soul. He's got a good father, of course, but it's not the same, is it? And Mr. Tremain's a busy man, and – well, it's never the same.'

The harbour was full of boats, some bobbing on the water, some drawn up on the shingle. Timothy pointed to one, lying at anchor near the mouth of the harbour. 'That's ours, the *Mylor*.'

When Jenny had come here before the Tremain craft had been a gleaming white yacht. This didn't look so new, schooner-rigged, a little over thirty feet, she reckoned. She said, 'I'd love to go sailing. I wonder if we might some time.'

Timothy watched a seagull, squinting at it with a concentration that camouflaged his troubled frown. 'I dunno,' he said reluctantly. 'Father doesn't always take anybody. He goes on his own most times.'

Jenny smiled. 'Never mind, there are lots of other things to do.' Timothy was not eager to sail and she wondered whether he was not sure Paul wanted him aboard until he said:

'That's the Witch's Rock,' and his voice shook.

The rock covered a small area but jutted high. It was over two miles out, but on a clear day you could see it from Tremain, even make out the pattern of it. It rose sheer above the waves facing the western seas, and sloping backwards towards the mainland until it curved in horseshoe shape, the inlet flattening to a tiny sandy cove.

According to the old story it was where the Tremain had caught the sea witch, and Jenny recalled it as a place of delight with its secret silver beach and its caves. At fifteen the caves had seemed to her pure magic, but Timothy didn't want to go to the Witch's Rock.

He turned his back on it now, and on the sea, and asked, 'Want to see Auntie Lorraine's shop?'

'Mmm, of *course*!' Jenny pretended great enthusiasm and she did want to see the shop, which was in a good spot towards the end of the harbour, next to an archway leading to what had once been a boat builders' yard and a row of cottages, but was now the artists' colony.

It was a double-fronted shop, displaying some saleable stuff: one or two pieces of stone sculpture, some pottery, a bone carved and polished until it looked like ivory, piskies in pottery and metal and wood; and pictures, a lot of pictures.

There were several people inside, looking around, and a woman in blue jeans and a scarlet shirt was sitting at a table towards the back of the shop, sketching with charcoal on a large white pad. She seemed intent on her work, but as Jenny and Timothy neared her she said, 'Hello, Timmy,' without looking up.

Timothy said, 'This is my Auntie Jenny,' and she looked up then. She had short greying hair and a tanned skin that made her teeth very white when she smiled. She said, 'I'm Grace Norbrook, I'm minding the store.'

She took the money for a piskie and popped him into a bag, said 'Thank you, do come again,' then turned back to Timothy. 'Leah and John are around somewhere. Have you come to play?'

Play would be fine, but Jenny was in charge of Timothy and a little apprehensive about letting him out of her sight. On the other hand he could surely come to no harm down here where everyone was his friend. Grace said with a smile, 'They're in the same gang. They go to school together.'

Timothy was going to boarding school next year. Jenny had thought that was a pity, but Caterine had said his name had been down practically from birth and boarding schools didn't come any better.

Now he looked longingly at the door and Jenny said, 'Shall we go and find them?'

'If you'll mind the shop,' Grace offered, 'I will.'

Jenny had never been a salesgirl, but she said, 'Fine,' and Grace went out through the side door that led to the courtyard.

Everything was priced, which made it simpler, and Jenny was completing the sale of a watercolour when

Grace came back with two youngsters of Timothy's age: a little girl, fair and stolid, and a boy, gipsy brown and thin.

Timothy introduced her again, 'This is my Auntie Jenny,' and the two children grinned at her. Grace Norbrook said:

'They know they mustn't go away, they're to stay down in the harbour, and how long can Timmy stay?'

'Oh, an hour,' said Jenny. Longer if they were having fun, because this was what Timothy needed. 'I'll sit on the harbour wall,' she said, 'and get myself a sun tan.' And watch Timothy. She mustn't be over-protective, but she would be happier keeping an eye on him.

The three children ran out together into the sunshine, going through the door in a squirming jumble, and Grace said, 'You don't mind, do you?'

'Of course not.'

'They get on well together, even when they're scrapping. And the roads are safe down here, no cars.'

She remembered and bit her lip and said, 'It was a terrible thing to happen.'

A whole town mourned for Caterine, wherever you turned. And there was nothing you could say, except, 'Yes, it was terrible.'

Grace asked, 'How's Lorraine?'

'Not too good yet,' Jenny admitted.

Someone bought a shell from a huge basket of shells and went out listening to it. Standing near to a window Jenny could see Timothy and his friends on the beach, walking with heads down, obviously searching. As Grace joined her again Jenny asked, 'What are they looking for?'

'This sort of thing.' Grace pointed towards a shelf of flotsam ware, root and branch sculptures. 'These were all found on the shore – John's father specializes in them. And Leah's mother does these.' She touched a paperweight of pearl pink shells and shining pebbles.

'Pretty,' said Jenny.

'For the tourists,' Grace smiled, and whispered, 'They sell better than the pictures.'

The shop seemed busy this morning, but it was brighter weather than for some time. Jenny asked, 'What sort of season have you had?'

'Fair,' said Grace. 'Tremain cottage industries get around. Everything pays its way around here.'

'That's good,' said Jenny, and Grace said:

'Yes, it is,' as though there were those who thought otherwise. 'Tell Lorraine we're coping, will you, although we'd like to see her back.'

'Does she run this place on her own?' Grace Norbrook could probably cope with half a dozen jobs and keep her cool, but Jenny would have expected Lorraine to dither under any sort of pressure.

'More or less,' said Grace. 'If there's a rush someone gives a hand, and if there's a special exhibition of course.'

'That surprises me,' said Jenny.

'Does it?' Grace sounded reflective. 'But perhaps you've only seen her up at Moidores.'

'I haven't seen her at all for a long time. Is she different at Moidores?'

The house overlooking the next cove also dominated the harbour. Even when the sun was shining, as it was now, the sea face of Moidores looked dark.

Grace laughed. 'I should think everyone is. Paul Tremain isn't the man to approve of a girl having her say, or doing her thing, is he?'

He had dictated Caterine's way of life, and Lorraine had less spirit and less strength than Caterine.

Jenny asked, 'What is Lorraine like down here?' and Grace said quickly:

'Don't get me wrong, I'm not saying she's a brilliant business woman. She can be put on and she can be cheated, but she does know a good picture when she sees it, and she works hard. Down here she makes her own decisions.' She added dryly, 'Mind you, if her brother thinks differently she soon changes them again.'

'You mean he has the final word?'

'In Tremain,' said Grace, 'Paul Tremain *is* the final word.'

'He sounds a thorough-going dictator.' Some of the resentment Jenny had always felt on Caterine's behalf came through, and Grace said:

'More benevolent feudal really. The maddening thing is he's usually right.' She laughed again and asked: 'How long are you staying?'

'I don't know.' Jenny moved round the side of the window display, almost pressing her cheek to the pane to watch Timothy, still with his friends, talking to someone by the harbour wall. 'As long as Timothy needs me.'

'He seems better than we'd heard.'

'The sun's shining,' said Jenny. 'It's storms that frighten him.'

Timothy spotted her behind the glass of the window and pointed, and the man with the children turned and stared. Jenny saw his face stiffen, and knew that it was her resemblance to Caterine again and drew back.

Grace was saying, 'Come down any time you need company. My house is the yellow door, third along, and the neighbours would be glad to see you.'

'Thank you,' Jenny murmured.

The man came into the shop. He was wiry, with black curly hair, wearing rope sandals, dingy slacks and a pink shirt open to the waist. He looked grave, but it was a face that would be attractive when he smiled.

'You're Jenny?' he said.

'Yes.'

'I'm Jack Bastaple.' Nobody had spoken of him to her, and he went on introducing himself as though he didn't expect the name to ring bells. 'I live here. That's mine.'

'That' was a painting, and Jenny looked as he indicated. Probably it was good, a dramatic study of sea and sky. He went on, 'Fancy a coffee or a drink?'

She hesitated. 'Thank you, but I came down with Timothy and I know he's all right, but—' she couldn't resist glancing back towards the window and Jack Bastaple said reassuringly:

'Of course he's all right. Anyhow, the pub has the sunshades out today, so we could sit there and watch the kids.'

They were all being kind to Caterine's sister, this and Grace inviting her round any time. Jenny said, 'That sounds pleasant,' and to Grace, 'I'll see you later?'

The Tremain Arms was central, where the road joined the quay. There were little tables outside and Jenny sat down while Jack Bastaple brought out two iced lagers.

He hadn't mentioned Caterine until he said, 'There is a likeness.'

'A slight one.'

He nodded, agreeing it was slight. 'I shouldn't think you were really alike, were you?'

The glasses were so cold they were misted. Caterine had been confident and cherished and beautiful and beloved. Jenny took a sip of cold amber liquid and said, 'No.'

He said quietly, 'She was enchanting.'

There we were not alike, thought Jenny wryly; I have never enchanted anyone in my life.

'It was such a waste,' he said. Then, with an obvious effort, he changed the subject. 'Tell me about yourself. What do you do for a living?'

'Shorthand and typing,' she said. 'What could be duller?' She hadn't found it dull, it depended on where and what, but he was looking at her and remembering Caterine and she had no illusions that he really wanted the story of her life. She turned the talk back to him. 'Have you lived here long?'

'I was born here.' So he must have been around when Jenny came four years ago. 'My father was a painter.'

'Was?'

'My parents died before the changeover.'

'What changeover?'

His voice was grim. 'When Paul Tremain took over.'

Jenny said without thinking:

'But I thought Tremain was always his,' and he laughed, the grimness dissolving.

'He's not *that* old.' Paul had been five years older than Caterine, of course that wasn't what she'd meant. 'The changeover after his father died. His father was a grand fellow. He'd have given you the coat off his back.'

'And Paul wouldn't?'

Jack Bastaple looked as though the lager had turned sour. 'I wouldn't care to be needing his coat unless I could offer a good price for it.'

'I gather you don't like him?'

'I liked his father.' He spoke with regret and affection. He looked at the little harbour. 'And I liked this place before the tourists came swarming, when the only boats out there were fishermen's boats.'

Some of the boats were probably fishing boats still, but there were launches now, luggers, ketches, yawls, a couple of yachts. 'My folk were poor,' he told her, 'but we were happy. If you couldn't raise the rent you knew it could wait. It didn't often have to wait because it wasn't much of a rent in those days.'

He sounded like an old man recalling old times, although he couldn't be out of his twenties. 'They were good days,' he said, and mourned them.

Jenny had never seen Tremain as the sleepy village of Jack Bastaple's boyhood, but she could understand him feeling that the visitors were intruders. As an intruder herself she was defensive. 'But they are customers. They do buy your paintings.'

'Sometimes,' he admitted grudgingly, glowering at a plump lady who was demanding shrilly and nasally of a plump gentleman taking a zooming ciné-picture. 'Hon, isn't this just the sweetest, quaintest little old place you have ever seen?'

Jenny held back a giggle. 'I think it's the sweetest too.'

'You do?' He frowned at her, and to him it was no laughing matter. Of course sweet was not the word. Down in the harbour now, in sunshine, with people in colourful holiday clothes, Tremain had a picture-postcard charm. But this was wrecker country, dangerous as the rocks under the shining water.

Out of season, in winter, it would be a very different place. Jenny said, 'I've never been here in the winter.'

She picked out Timothy's bright blue T-shirt near the end of the jetty where one of the pleasure boats was moored. His friends were still with him. The stolid-looking little girl was skipping up and down, the boys were talking to the man who was helping passengers into the boat.

Jack asked, 'Are you going to be here in winter?'

'I shouldn't think so.' This was the first week of August. 'I should think I'll be gone long before then.'

'If you escape.'

She turned to stare at him. '*What?*'

His eyes took her gaze out to the Witch's Rock. He said, 'This Tremain would never have let the sea witch get away.'

'What does that mean?'

'Moidores was a golden prison to Caterine. If you have any talents they'll die in that house. Tremain will see to that. Caterine wasted her gifts.'

'I know.' It seemed everyone knew, and to a dedicated artist wasting your gifts would be a betrayal. 'But it was Caterine's choice and she *was* happy.'

'She might have been happier.'

Of course she might, if she could have had the best of both worlds. But she had counted her career well lost for love and she hadn't regretted it. Jenny said:

'What's the use of talking like this now?' What could be more futile? 'And it was never any use talking. It was Caterine's choice.'

'You've never tried fighting Tremain, have you?'

'No.'

'The rocks out there are easier to move than him.' Some of this bitterness could be for Caterine, but some was surely for himself, and Jenny heard herself say:

'You hate him, don't you?'

That checked him. He sat silent for a morose moment, then he denied it. 'No, I don't hate him.' A few more seconds and he smiled, 'It's just that I would like to see someone stand up to him for once and get away with it.'

Behind that statement she sensed years of frustration. 'In Tremain Paul Tremain *is* the final word,' Grace had said.

Jenny smiled too, 'You don't mean me,' and he laughed

with her and patted her hand on the table.

'Oh no, not you.'

He meant she would stand no chance, she was no use for moving rocks, and he could well be right. But she could leave Moidores whenever she chose, and while she stayed Paul Tremain was making no rules for her.

The children were coming from the jetty, running along by the harbour wall, heading for the Tremain Arms, and Jenny leaned forward anxiously because they weren't smiling.

As they reached her Leah said firmly, 'Timothy can go round the bay, can't he?'

John explained, 'In the *White Wave*. It isn't full and Jim says we can go, only Tim says you mightn't let him.'

Timothy hadn't spoken. Now he said jerkily, 'I said I think we've got to go home.' He was not breathless, he was holding his breath. A pleasure trip with his friends on a lovely day could have been the ideal way of dispelling his fears of the sea. But if there was any risk of panic his friends mustn't see it, his pride was precious to him.

Jenny glanced at her watch and said, 'I'm afraid we must. We have to look in the shop again, and then we do have to go home.'

Leah and John scowled at her, the villain of the piece, the spoilsport. They were sorry for Timothy being lumbered with her.

Jack Bastaple got up and said, 'I'll walk back with you.' The children followed. Jenny heard Timothy say in answer to Leah's mutter:

'She is *not*! She's all right.'

Just outside the crafts shop Leah and John scampered away, back towards the jetty, and Timothy stood by the window looking through the glass into the shop.

He wasn't seeing the goods for sale, Jenny knew. He was scared, and he was scared that his friends would guess. Her heart ached for him because at seven years of age, after what had happened, anyone – including stolid little Leah – would understand why he feared the sea. He shouldn't need pride at seven years of age.

Grace was serving. Jack joined a couple who were viewing the paintings, and told them that the artist they fancied but considered pricey had exhibited in last year's Academy. They looked as though that might tip the balance.

Jenny examined the shells marked 'All at 25p' in the basket by the door. She could see Timothy without looking at him directly, and as she poked carefully around he came inside and looked down with her.

He said, 'You don't want to buy them. You can pick them up on the beach.'

Jenny smiled. If Jack Bastaple heard that he would certainly think Timothy spoke as his father's son, although in Jenny's experience Paul Tremain was far from tight-fisted and Timothy loved giving.

'All right,' she said. 'You show me where to find them.'

Grace went to the door with her customers, who now wanted to see a Cornish tin mine. She was giving them directions how to get there, and she stepped outside to finish. She came back, smiling. 'We're having a busy morning. Jenny, you've brought the sunshine. And the trade.'

'I only hope I can keep it up,' said Jenny. 'We're off home now. Is there anything you want me to tell Lorraine, anything I can take up for you?' While Grace was considering she added, 'It might be a good idea,' and Grace nodded, understanding.

'Ah yes – well, there's some correspondence here I'd set on one side for Mr. Morrison.'

Joseph Morrison, Paul's personal assistant. Jenny remembered him as a grey man: grey hair, grey suit, grey eyes. He had been middle-aged, he would still be middle-aged, very quiet and efficient.

Grace brought a large envelope out of a room at the back of the shop and said, 'If Lorraine isn't up to it, give them to Mr. Morrison, would you?'

Jack Bastaple walked with them to the gates of Moidores, and watched them down the drive and into the house. On his way back to Tremain he came again to the curve in the road where Caterine's car had skidded. With Jenny and Timothy he had passed it without a glance, but now he left the road and crossed the rough turf to the cliff's edge. He stood there for a long time. . . .

Ebby was in the kitchen and Jenny left Timothy with her and went to find Lorraine. Lorraine was in the drawing-room, sitting at the little Georgian writing bureau with an open diary. As Jenny walked in she said, 'It's Caterine's. There should have been a dinner party on Saturday.'

Caterine had loved entertaining, Jenny knew. She was a wonderful hostess, she had had so many friends. Lorraine said desolately, 'It's so quiet without her. I keep expecting her to walk in, or I find myself listening for her.' She tilted her head as though she was listening now and Jenny put down the envelope on top of the desk diary.

'Grace asked me to bring you that. Grace Norwood.'

'You met Grace?' Lorraine looked at the envelope, making no attempt to open it.

'In the shop. And Jack Bastaple.' As Lorraine said nothing Jenny went on, 'I don't remember either of them, but Jack was born here, wasn't he? I don't think I met him before. Was Grace here then?'

'No. She and her husband came just after you stopped coming.'

'I liked the shop,' said Jenny. She talked about the customers she had seen this morning, and asked about the artists, and from brief replies Lorraine gradually became more expansive. When Jenny said, 'Grace said if you didn't want to bother with these I was to give them to Mr. Morrison,' Lorraine tipped the contents of the envelope on to the desk and said:

'I'd better see what they are.'

Lunch was a light meal, eaten round the kitchen table with Eb and Ebby, and Dolly the daily who lived in Tremain. Paul was rarely in to lunch, Jenny was told, and when she was down at the shop often as not neither was Lorraine.

Lorraine said that tomorrow she would be going down

to Tremain, and after lunch she went back to the papers Jenny had brought for her.

Jenny and Timothy spent the afternoon in the cove below Moidores. The only way down was the iron steps fixed in the cliff face, and for that you needed fitness and a head for heights. Jenny was fit enough, but she closed her eyes while she was on the steps and felt rock under her feet with remembered relief.

Once down it was worth the effort. The tide was going out, leaving behind wet shingle and cool rocks, and little pools each a tiny watery world. They clambered over the rocks and peered into the pools and Jenny felt as young as Timothy. He knew more about the seashore than she did. He knew the names of the weeds and the creatures, this had been his playground all his life.

The sun shone as they ran and splashed at the water's edge. Timothy was a good swimmer, but he didn't swim this afternoon, so Jenny said, 'You'll have to teach me some time, I don't swim as well as you do.'

'All right,' said Timothy. 'Do you like being here?' He spoke smugly, it *was* his cove, and Jenny's delight in it was immense. She felt a content that glowed warmer than the sun on her skin, and when they had to leave, and Timothy scrambled ahead up the cliff face, she was relaxed and refreshed. Sea air suited her. It made her a new woman.

Paul didn't join them that evening. After dinner, with Timothy in bed, Jenny and Lorraine sat watching television and talking. Lorraine seemed more relaxed too, although whether that was tranquillizers or whether the work Grace had sent her had helped Jenny couldn't know.

She talked about the shop. She was proud of it, she enjoyed it, and she was going down tomorrow 'for a little while at any rate'. But she still looked very pale and her eyes were still full of shadows.

She went to bed quite early, before Jenny, and Jenny spent the next hour with Ebby and Eb in the big old-fashioned kitchen. She liked this room, she always had. She was more at home in the kitchen, and that was a fact,

46

just as Caterine's natural setting had always been the elegant rooms.

But the Ebsworths kept early hours too, and when their bedtime came Jenny was still wakeful. She said good night to them, then went upstairs and looked in on Timothy, then came downstairs again and watched the end of the television programmes.

This room faced the sea and when she turned off the TV set Jenny drew back the curtains and looked out. There was a moon tonight, silhouetting the dark outline of the land, silvering the water, and to a girl used to shut-in city streets it was breathtaking.

She turned an armchair to face the window and sat and watched the stars, motionless in the sky, dancing in the sea. She thought – and smiled at herself – no wonder the sea witch swam away; because this was enchantment. It turned the softness of the armchair into a cloud that floated along a silver road, out to the rock maybe. You couldn't see the rock, but it was there, and it was terrifyingly beautiful.

She could have stayed for hours. She did stay longer than she thought, perhaps she fell asleep. She was startled when a clock on a side table struck one.

She put the chair back in place again, and made her way out of the room. The house was quiet, it was such a vast place that it was eerie when there was no sound but the sound of the sea.

From the gallery she looked down into the hall, and saw a diffused lighting from the closed door of the office, and sighed as she went on towards her bedroom.

Paul couldn't be working this late, and he shouldn't be up still, particularly after last night. But Jenny couldn't intrude again. It was no business of hers. She was the last one in this house with the right to concern herself.

Eb or Ebby, who had been here since Paul was a boy, might have opened that door and said, 'This is doing no good. This is only the way to make yourself ill.'

Lorraine could have taken in a cup of coffee. She was her sister, he was her concern. He might be tough, but he couldn't go on like this.

As she reached Lorraine's door Jenny hesitated, then tapped very lightly. It wouldn't have woken anyone, but Lorraine was awake, she called at once, 'Yes?'

'It's Jenny.'

'What is it?'

Jenny went in. 'I fell asleep downstairs. It's after one o'clock and Paul's still in the office.'

Lorraine wriggled herself into a hunched shape, her pale face turned to Jenny. 'Is he?'

Jenny said, 'He can't be working, can he?'

'I don't know. He's often up late.'

One o'clock was nothing, but Jenny said, 'I don't think he went to bed at all last night. I woke and I thought it was Timmy in Caterine's room, but it was Paul and that was after three o'clock. He was just standing there.'

'You're his sister. Couldn't you go in to him?'

'*No!*' She sounded as though she cowered as she spoke, and she must know Paul and that no one must offer him compassion.

Jenny said, 'I'm sorry, I didn't mean to interfere, I just felt sorry.'

'He loved Caterine,' said Lorraine.

'I know.'

Lorraine said in a whisper in the darkness, 'He loved her, but in a way I suppose he killed her.'

CHAPTER THREE

'*Killed* her?' Jenny echoed shrilly, and Lorraine said:

'I didn't mean it like that. At least—' She was biting her lip and Jenny demanded:

'What did you mean?'

'I shouldn't have said that.'

But she had said it and it had to be explained. Jenny pressed the button on the tiny bedside lamp and Lorraine put a hand over her eyes and turned her head, and Jenny felt like a bullying interrogator, but she had to know. She pleaded, 'Please tell me.'

'There'd been a quarrel.' Lorraine's voice was muffled. 'Caterine was terribly upset.'

'She seemed all right when I spoke to her.'

'She was an actress, wasn't she?' Of course she could have hidden her distress for those few moments on the telephone. Lorraine said dully, 'She'd had a row with Paul, that was why she decided to visit you, it was all on the spur of the moment.'

That explained why Caterine wouldn't wait till morning, and why she had driven with too little care.

Lorraine said, 'I'd never seen her cry before.' Nor had Jenny, even when their parents died. 'I suppose this time she'd thought it would be different, with Timmy getting older, she really had thought Paul would let her do some acting again, but he wouldn't even discuss it.'

So sacrificing her career had mattered to Caterine. She had tried to fight for the chance to use her talents, and Paul wouldn't even discuss it. Like Jack Bastaple had said – like the rocks, as unmoving and uncaring.

Now he cared. Now it was too late. He had loved her in his fashion, but she had driven that car along the cliff road, weeping for the first time in her life because of him.

It was still an accident, but it should never have happened.

Jenny said bitterly, 'So it isn't just grief that won't let him sleep, it's conscience.'

'I think it is,' Lorraine whispered. 'And for me too. I wish I'd at least tried to say something to Paul, or tried to stop Caterine driving for a while.' She was almost wringing her hands. 'Oh, I do wish I'd *tried*!'

'It wasn't your fault. Anybody can be wise afterwards.' And neither Paul nor Caterine would have listened to anything Lorraine had tried to say. She seemed grateful that Jenny wasn't blaming her.

'I didn't really have a chance. She phoned you and she threw a few things into a case, kissed Timmy good-bye and told Ebby she'd decided to have a few days' holiday. She was laughing again then, they'd no idea.'

A grim thought struck Jenny. 'Timmy didn't know about the quarrel?'

'No, he was with Ebby.'

'Thank goodness for that!' Jenny wished she hadn't known herself. Bitterness choked her so that when Lorraine said:

'I don't think he'll ever forgive himself,' she said savagely,

'I hope he never can.'

'Please don't,' Lorraine implored. 'You make things hard enough as it is.'

'Why?'

Lorraine sat aureoled in the soft spotlight of the table lamp, looking at Jenny in the shadows. 'You're much more like Caterine than you used to be. When I saw you first I thought – Jenny's like Caterine's ghost. We shall be living with Caterine's ghost.'

There was more than a touch of hysteria in that and Jenny said flatly, 'I'm no ghost, I promise you.'

She turned to go and Lorraine called beseechingly after her, 'You won't say anything about what I've told you will you?'

'Of course I won't. Who would I tell it to?'

She went through the nursery into her own room. Timothy was sleeping, but the faint click of the connecting door disturbed him and he murmured, not quite awake,

'Auntie Jen?'

'Hush, Timmy, I've just come to bed.'

He didn't look at her and see Caterine now. She was no ghost for Timmy. She was the security that comforted him and sent him back to sleep.

She wished Lorraine had not told her about the quarrel. She didn't want to feel revengeful. Paul was hating himself, allowing himself no peace. He had had to identify Caterine and live with the fact that he was partly responsible, and remembering that Jenny could almost pity him. Almost but not quite. Not yet. . . .

She came down to breakfast next morning with Timothy running ahead. They were early, but Paul was finishing his meal as they went into the breakfast-room.

He looked as usual. He said good morning to Jenny and hello to Timothy. Jenny took a seat. Timothy stayed by Paul to tell him about going down to Tremain yesterday, and to the cove in the afternoon, and that he was 'going to teach Auntie Jen to swim because she doesn't swim as good as me.'

'That sounds an excellent idea,' said Paul. He drained his cup while the child chattered on, then Timothy said:

'I'll tell Ebby,' and skipped away towards the kitchen.

'More coffee?' asked Jenny.

'No, thank you.'

She poured herself a cup and as Paul got up she heard herself say, 'You worked late last night.' The dark eyebrows raised a fraction. 'There was a light on in the office, very late.'

She looked back at him steadily. She hoped he was lonely. His possessiveness had helped to kill Caterine.

He said quietly, 'You don't appear to be keeping early hours yourself. Excuse me.' And left her feeling ashamed of that urge to put hurt on hurt. . . .

Eb was going over to Blades, the home farm, this morning, and Timothy was going with him. 'Want to come?' asked Timmy, and Jenny almost said, 'I'd like to,' but there was no real need for her to go along. Eb would look after Timmy, and if Jenny went it would only be for her own pleasure.

She was not on holiday here. She was taking no salary, but she was living under Paul's roof at his expense, and after last night that was distasteful to her. Being with Timmy was not earning her keep, that was for love, she didn't count that, but there must always be scope for another pair of hands in a house the size of Moidores.

She asked Ebby, 'Can I help you this morning?'

'If you like,' said Ebby cheerfully, 'if you've nothing better to do.'

Jenny started with the washing up and Dolly, arriving on the dot of nine, was surprised to find her at the sink. Dolly, a plump and pretty little widow in her late thirties, hadn't said much at lunch yesterday, but sharing a sink seemed to bring out her mateyness and as she dried the dishes she told Jenny about her son, who was starting as a medical student at Exeter in September.

She was fetching out the snapshots when Ebby came back into the kitchen and said, 'Bedrooms this morning, Dolly,' so Dolly replaced the snaps in her handbag and went to the broom cupboard to collect the vacuum cleaner.

Jenny asked, 'Can I help with the bedrooms?'

'No,' said Ebby, and Dolly went off on her own, humming to herself. 'Get that one talking about young Andrew,' said Ebby when the door had closed, 'and there'll be no work done.'

'He sounds a nice boy. No wonder she's proud of him.'

'He's all right,' Ebby conceded. 'He turned out all right.'

'Good,' said Jenny. 'Now what do I do?'

Ebby thought about it. 'Well, lunch will be cold meat. Probably no Mr. Paul again, and we shan't know what milady's doing until she turns up or she doesn't turn up.'

She meant Lorraine, who had gone down to Tremain. Jenny said, 'I hope she stays at the shop.'

'Let's hope she does,' Ebby agreed emphatically. 'She needs to be getting about again. You could do the vegetables for tonight.'

While Jenny scraped potatoes and sliced runner beans Ebby set out the baking ingredients on the kitchen table, and creamed away in the big mixing bowl.

Sunlight streamed through the windows and Ebby said suddenly, 'Why don't you go down to the beach? We haven't had that much sunshine this summer, it's a shame to waste it.'

It was a temptation and Jenny smiled, 'I can't treat Moidores like a free hotel.'

Ebby looked shocked. 'I should hope not.' Hotel indeed! You're part of the family.'

'Not really,' said Jenny. She didn't really belong, either in Moidores or Tremain. She said quietly, 'From what I heard yesterday Paul expects most things to pay their way round here, so perhaps I'd better work for my supper.'

'Please yourself.' Ebby gave the already smooth mixture another bout of fast beating. Then she said sharply, 'Talking of working, some of them think it's easy for him because he's Tremain. If anyone starts on that tack you can tell them he works his eyes out.'

Jenny was being scolded for sounding priggish, and because Ebby suspected she had listened to criticism of Paul Tremain without leaping to his defence. Ebby was completely satisfied with the way Paul managed his affairs, and it would have been useless for Jenny to say, 'He works hard because he enjoys it. Being a tycoon is his life. So why couldn't he agree that Caterine's work should be a tiny part of her life?'

It would have been useless, and cruel, and wrong. . . . No one had the right to sit in judgment, and Caterine had been happy. Paul had been kind to her, he had given her almost everything. He had loved her, but his last sight of the living Caterine had been of tears, and his last words to her had been harsh, and that was enough for a man to bear.

Pity finally overwhelmed Jenny's bitterness. Paul wouldn't take pity, but someone in this household should make him see sense. She said, 'He was still in the office last night after one o'clock. I fell asleep watching television, and I saw the office light still on.'

Ebby sieved flour, salt and spices very carefully into the bowl. Jenny said, 'I think someone should have suggested it was time he stopped working.'

'Do you?' Ebby's mouth went down at the corners. 'Who?'

'I asked Lorraine to go in to him.' Ebby shook her head, she knew Lorraine. Jenny said, 'She wouldn't. Would you have done?'

'Why didn't you?' said Ebby. 'He can't sack you.' That was a wry joke, Jenny couldn't imagine the Ebsworths ever being at risk. What Ebby meant was that she wasn't interfering and Jenny asked bluntly,

'How much grieving does he think he can take? I don't believe he slept at all the night before, he was walking around the house at three o'clock in the morning, and if he does crack up what happens to Timothy?'

'He won't let Timmy down,' said Ebby. She went on with her cake mixing. 'Nor any of us,' she said firmly. 'He'll bear the load.'

She meant that Paul was a rock. As Jack Bastaple had said, but not in the way Jack had meant it. A man seen by two who were dependent on him, one accepting, one resenting.

But no man was rock. Paul Tremain was flesh and blood and he could break. Lorraine hadn't the strength to stand up against him even if it was for his good; and Ebby believed he was still in control. To Ebby this was simply natural grief, she didn't know about the quarrel, the load was heavier than she suspected.

For Timothy's sake he had to carry on. He wouldn't turn Jenny out of Moidores, because of Timothy. He certainly wouldn't listen to her advice, but if she had taken coffee to the office last night she would at least have disturbed his vigil, and next time she might do that.

She dusted and carpet-swept the drawing-room, drawn again and again to the windows that overlooked the bay and sea. It was another fine day, with any luck the tourists would be trooping into Tremain, and customers in the shop might tempt Lorraine into getting down to work again.

There were boats on the water, but the cove below Moidores was deserted, and this afternoon when Timmy was back Jenny hoped he would choose the lonely cove.

They might start their swimming lessons. That would get him into the sea again; she knew he had loved it before the accident. They had never been to swimming pools when Timothy and Caterine had come on holiday to Jenny's home, and he was too young to remember Jenny's visits here. That was as well, it meant he didn't know that Jenny swam far better than he did.

Mid-morning Dolly and Ebby stopped for a ten-minute cup of tea, and Jenny took in Mr. Morrison's tray: one cup of almost black coffee and two arrowroot biscuits.

He was standing by an open drawer of a filing cabinet going through a file, and he looked round with a faint fleeting surprise. Joseph Morrison had not changed. His hair had always been grey in Jenny's memory. The lines were not marked in his face because he never allowed himself more than minimal movement of facial muscles. She could never recall hearing him laugh or his voice raised, or seeing him scowl deeply or smile widely.

Caterine had not liked him. She had admitted his intelligence, he was a wizard with figures and accounts, who knew more about Paul Tremain's affairs than anyone else. And he had given Caterine the creeps.

'He's so grey,' she had said to Jenny more than once. 'Like a shadow. I don't think there's any blood in him. When he looks at you with those cold eyes of his you feel he can thought-read, and I wouldn't put that past him.'

Joseph Morrison had been the only person in Moidores and Tremain for whom Caterine had had an active antipathy. She had made fun of most of them, but never of him. It was almost as though she was a little afraid of him, and once when Jenny had said, 'If he worked for Paul's father he must be getting on, isn't he due to retire?' Caterine had snorted:

'Paul wouldn't let him retire, he'll be there for ever.

Paul likes the wretched man, he wouldn't hear a word against him.'

Now he took the tray from Jenny. 'Good morning, Miss Douglas.'

'Good morning,' said Jenny.

She might have been in this room years ago, but she couldn't remember it, and she took in quickly the impression of office cabinets and wall graphs, in and out trays, a couple of phones, two desks – one very slightly the larger.

Mr. Morrison had a typewriter on his desk, the same make that Jenny had used in her last temporary post. She gave it a light pat. 'They're good, aren't they?'

'We have always found it satisfactory,' he told her.

There was nothing in the machine, and presumably he was going to drink his coffee and eat his biscuits, so it would be standing idle for a few minutes and Jenny asked, 'May I try it?'

'Certainly.'

She typed a few lines, and looked up to see what was surely the glimmer of a smile. She couldn't think what was amusing him, he was the last man in whom she would have expected humour.

He coughed at her inquiring expression. 'Forgive me, but it seems a most unlikely thing that a sister of Mrs. Tremain should be typing so efficiently.'

Jenny's lips curved. They did have that surface semblance, and the idea of Caterine tapping away at a typewriter was ridiculous. It was the spotlight for Caterine and the applause, in everyday life as well. Caterine was born to dazzle.

Jenny said ruefully, 'I suppose I am an unlikely kind of sister.'

She could see what Caterine had meant about Mr. Morrison's scrutiny, but she did not go along with Caterine's opinion all the way. She would not have said that the grey eyes were cold. Piercing, yes, and very clear, but to Jenny it was not a chilling gaze. She said, on impulse, 'You know that Paul asked me to come down to be with Timothy?'

'Yes.' His voice conveyed regret for the circumstances, he didn't add anything.

'I would very much like to earn my keep while I'm here. I suppose you have a secretary already?'

'At the mine.'

The tin mine was only part of the Tremain estate, there must be plenty of paper work connected with other property and industries. 'Who does the typing here?' Jenny asked.

'Some we take over to the general office, some I do myself. It's a simple matter to recruit staff during the summer, but in the winter they usually decide to go inland.'

She could believe that Mr. Morrison would prefer to do the work himself rather than face a constant change-over of staff. She said, 'I shall only be here for a month or so, but if you could find me something to do I would be grateful. It would help me keep up my speeds, and I am used to office work. Anything.'

'Have you discussed this with Mr. Tremain?'

'I didn't think about it until now.'

'Then I suggest that you do.' But he sounded as though he would raise no objections, and, encouraged, she asked:

'Is there anything I could do now, so that I could show Paul something? Unless it's all top secret.'

Again that faint smile. 'This is not MI5 headquarters,' said Mr. Morrison, and Jenny giggled, realizing incredulously – but he's nice.

'Can you understand this?' He pushed across some pages in a crabbed handwriting, referring to repairs on property, that had been lying on his desk. Jenny glanced through them.

'I think so.'

She looked into the kitchen to tell Ebby, who said, 'If you're going to work in the office the next night Mr. Paul stays up too late you'll be able to go in and tell him won't you?'

'I might at that,' said Jenny with a small grimace, and Ebby laughed.

She made a workmanlike job of the copy-typing. The writing, which she guessed was Mr. Morrison's, was so small and closely packed it was almost illegible at times. And he had his own abbreviations that took getting used to, but she worked her way through without asking for help.

She was on the last page when he said, 'I shall be in the library for the next five minutes if there should be any phone calls.'

'Right,' said Jenny. She was reaching the trickiest para-graph of all, over-written in places, where a magnifying glass would have come in handy.

She sat frowning down, unwilling to give up here, as though she had come to the last pieces in a complicated jigsaw puzzle. It had become a challenge to decipher the darn thing to the end, but whether these words or those went first nobody but the man who had written them could say, and when he came back she was still unde-cided.

She tried it out again in her mind and Paul asked pleasantly, 'Going through the accounts?'

'Oh!' She jerked up, surprise making her idiotic. 'What are you doing here?'

He didn't bother to answer that and she explained, 'Mr. Morrison's in the library. I was typing this out – I asked him if he could find me some work.'

'Are you bored already?'

'*No.*'

'Where's Timothy?'

'He went with Eb to Blades. He'll be all right with Eb.'

'I'm sure he will.' There was irony in Paul's voice, he had hardly needed Jenny to reassure him about Alec Ebsworth, and she said:

'I mean, Timothy doesn't need me as well this morn-ing. I don't think he needs me to be around all the time so long as I'm near for a while.' The words were getting tangled. She went on, 'He's an independent little boy, he's very proud, he's been taking care of me, right from the beginning when Rolf Perrie brought him to me.'

She was proud of Timothy. To hide his own fear and to feel for others was a marvellous thing in a child so young. She said, 'He is a super kid.'

'You could be prejudiced,' said Paul. He smiled at her.

'I could,' she agreed. 'But he's still a super kid.'

Mr. Morrison came back, carrying a thick book that looked like a directory, and Paul said, 'I see we're increasing the staff.' Mr. Morrison picked up a typewritten page, gave it a brief glance and handed it to Paul.

Paul exclaimed 'Good lord!' He was obviously surprised, and Jenny's voice had a tinge of huffiness. It was no compliment he should have expected her to produce second-rate work. She said coolly:

'I have had training, and some experience.'

He picked up a second page. 'So had the others,' he said. 'But you're the first in six years who could read Joe's writing.'

She smiled. Mr. Morrison said, 'A slight exaggeration, but I think we should avail ourselves of Miss Douglas's offer of help while she is here.'

Somehow, instinctively, she knew that Paul did not want her working with him and she said, 'I wouldn't neglect Timothy, but I am going to have time on my hands.'

'There are pleasanter ways of passing your time. Why do you want to spend it cooped up in here?'

She explained, 'Because when I go home I shall have to look around for a job again. I was very out of touch, it had been a long time. I'm not so bad now, but I still need practice.'

Paul's expression was not encouraging, and she turned to Mr. Morrison, who met her pleading eyes with a look of blank non-committal. No further support seemed to be coming from him and she demanded of both of them, 'Why not? I could do a couple of hours in the morning while Timothy's still on holiday, maybe help with the mail.'

A very small nod from Mr. Morrison, nothing from Paul, and she wailed at Paul, 'Well, you could give me a

59

try. If I'm no use you won't have lost anything, and if I am I wouldn't want paying. I just want to feel I'm earning my keep.'

He said flatly, 'If you worked for me you'd certainly be paid.'

Jenny didn't want his money. Her mouth set and she began, 'I don't—' He spoke quietly, cutting across her words.

'I wouldn't care to be in your debt any more than you want to be in mine.'

She realized then how petty she was being, considering she had lived for years on the allowance he had paid her mother. Making amends with a spark of mischief she smiled, 'All right, it's a deal,' and after a moment he laughed.

She consolidated her advantage, turning businesslike. 'Just this line, Mr. Morrison, I'm not quite sure.' He told her what came first, and she typed it, not looking at Paul again, hoping the laugh meant he was relenting.

Morrison watched her typing and asked, 'Do you take shorthand, Miss Douglas?'

'Yes.'

'Capital.' He dictated another paragraph, completing the report, and she got it down easily; he was not a fast talker. She was starting to type it when Timothy walked in.

He looked for Jenny first, and seeing her behind the typewriter grinned. Then he looked at Paul. 'Hello, Father. Auntie Jen, do you want me to teach you to ride?'

'Not very much,' said Jenny. 'I'd rather you taught me to swim.'

'Oh, I'll do that.' That was settled and needed no further discussion. 'But Snowy's a quiet horse.'

'Good,' said Jenny, 'but is Snowy a little horse? Because when Auntie Lorraine tried to teach me I kept falling off.'

Timmy blew out his cheeks while he thought about it, then decided, 'A bit little.'

'Near to the ground and very wide,' said Paul, his deep

60

voice not quite steady, and Jenny said gaily:

'Made to measure. O.K., Timmy, I'll learn to ride. I'm doing some typing now, I'll be finished in a few minutes.'

'Oright,' said Timmy, adding nonchalantly, 'I'll teach you to swim this afternoon if you like.'

'He expects a quick pupil,' said Paul when the door closed. Then he spoke without laughter. 'I am in your debt.'

Jenny said quickly, 'No. I'm getting more than I'm giving for the—' She bit her lip; she had been going to say, 'for the first time in my life.' The unspoken words hung in the air and both men heard them.

She began to type again, and Paul said to Mr. Morrison, 'Perrie will be along this afternoon about Branch Three, I've brought the papers with me.'

He took files out of a briefcase and they were deep in them when Jenny paper-clipped her report together and placed it beside the typewriter, then stood up.

Mr. Morrison looked up, Paul didn't, and Jenny said softly, 'Nine o'clock in the morning?' He gave his faint smile and she got out of the room quickly. Paul hadn't said 'No' and that was good enough.

After lunch Jenny and Timmy went down to the cove below Moidores. This time Jenny ran for the water's edge. She hadn't swum in the sea for years, but if she had been alone she would have struck off for one of the distant rocks, perhaps even the Witch's Rock.

She could swim without tiring almost indefinitely. Water seemed her natural element. She delighted in the cool caress of it against her skin, the feel of it lifting her hair; and in the shallows now she longed to slip into deeper waters and swim away.

She was a very quick pupil. They swam a short distance from the shore with Timothy circling and splashing around her like a protective porpoise. Then they picked their way back over the stones – Jenny needed sandals but the soles of Timothy's feet were leather tough – and climbed the cliffside steps back to the house.

Jenny said, 'That was lovely, I had a lovely swim,' and

Timothy said:

'You're not bad, Auntie Jen, but you'd better get dressed now because you're not used to it and you'll catch cold.'

She wasn't cold. She was glowing beneath her swimsuit and Lorraine's towel jacket. She had borrowed the jacket this morning. Lorraine had said, 'Timmy's teaching *you* to swim?' and when Jenny explained had agreed it was a good idea to get him playing in the sea again. 'The children round here live in it all summer long.'

Timmy had swum well out of his depth today, watching Jenny who reached for him sometimes, pretending she needed help but always smiling so that he laughed too.

The sea with the sun on it had had no fears for him, but the sun had not shone when Caterine died. When the storms came again the terror might seize him, but today Jenny felt they had taken a little hurdle.

Rolf Perrie was in the kitchen when she came down from bathing and changing. She had left Timothy in his room, setting up a train set which he had unearthed from one of the cupboards, and which seemed to have enough track to cover the entire floor of his room and probably of hers as well.

Rolf was sitting by the kitchen range and Ebby had a trayful of brasses on the table. She had reached the polishing stage and most of them gleamed.

Jenny said hello to Rolf, and to Ebby, 'Timmy's putting out his train set.' Ebby rolled her eyes in mock resignation and Jenny commented, 'There seems to be a lot of it.'

'There is a lot of it,' said Ebby dolefully.

Jenny's hair was still damp, plastered to her head, and she told Rolf unnecessarily, 'We've been swimming, Timmy and me.'

'It's all right for some,' said Rolf. The tension that had aged him the night he brought Timmy to her had gone now. He looked his right age, and he was a good-looking young man with a sensitive face.

'Isn't it just?' said Jenny, and asked Ebby, 'By the way,

has Lorraine come back?'

'No.' Ebby admired a candlestick at arm's length, breathed on one spot and gave it another rub. It was almost six, the time the shop would be shutting, so Lorraine had seen the day through and that was good.

Rolf Perrie got up. 'I'd better be getting along.' He still lived on his parents' farm, although he was now the manager of the tin mine. Jenny said:

'Remember me to your folk.'

'I will.'

'And tell your mother Timmy's determined I'm going to learn to ride, but if I come past your farm I'll try not to fall off into the pigsties again.'

Rolf laughed, 'I'll tell her, but she'd be pleased to see you.'

A bell rang in the glass-fronted case of bells high on the wall, making Jenny jump. 'Shall I go?' she offered. 'Which room is it?'

'The office. It's all right.' Ebby gave her hands a quick swill under the tap and dried them fast. The moment he and Jenny were alone Rolf asked:

'How is Lorraine?'

The query seemed casual, but why hadn't he asked the people better placed to tell him than Jenny? Ebby or Paul. 'She went down to the shop this morning,' said Jenny. 'She must have stayed there. At least I suppose she must.'

'How did she seem to you?'

'Very upset. But that's to be expected, isn't it?'

'Of course.'

If he wanted to know how Lorraine was there was a surer way than asking questions. 'If you wait a little she'll be back,' Jenny suggested. 'Or you could go and meet her.'

Rolf said, 'No, I'd better be on my way.'

'Any message?'

'No. Thank you.' He looked up at the bells. 'That's Tremain,' he said. 'Press a bell and somebody jumps. You did, didn't you, like Ebby and me? Caterine wouldn't have done. Nor Lorraine.'

Jenny resisted an impulse to say 'So what?' and said instead, 'No message for Lorraine?'

'No,' said Rolf for the third time.

All the same when Lorraine came back to Moidores half an hour later Jenny said, 'Rolf Perrie was asking after you.'

'Was he?' said Lorraine. 'That was nice of him.' Then she began to tell Jenny about a couple who had come into the shop today, and bought every flattish shell in stock to set in white cement on a patio wall.

They had had lunch at the Tremain Arms while Grace and Lorraine sent out all the local children on a shell hunt, and came back after lunch for the spoils, nearly three hundred shells in all.

Lorraine was more animated than Jenny had seen her. She told the tale amusingly and she seemed to have had a busy day.

Jenny had a full day too. Paul was home for dinner tonight. They ate in the dining-room, and Jenny remembered Caterine at this table. They must all be remembering Caterine, recalling the candle-flames dancing and the faces of guests, and Caterine holding court. And family meals like this, but Caterine here.

Paul was silent. Timothy chattered and Lorraine talked a little, and Jenny sat between them keeping the talk going and a façade of normality.

After dinner it was bedtime for Timmy, but they played with the train set for a while, Timmy in pyjamas showing Jenny how to work the controls. And when he was snuggled down in bed she stayed in her own room, moving quietly around so that he knew she was near. He was sound asleep quite soon.

As she passed the door of Caterine's room she tried the knob. The door was locked and she was glad of that.

Downstairs in the drawing-room Lorraine sat with her feet up on a Louis Quinze sofa, her silver fair hair spilling over a dark red velvet cushion. As Jenny walked into the room she asked fearfully, 'Did you have any trouble?'

'Trouble?'

'With Timmy.'

'No, he's asleep.'

Lorraine was looking strained again, and she closed her eyes letting out a soft breath of relief. 'He hardly slept at all before Paul sent him up to you, and when he did when he woke he'd run into Caterine's room.'

Since he had had Jenny near he had not run. Jenny said, 'I think he'll sleep, he's tired. And Caterine's door's locked – that's as well, isn't it?'

Lorraine's eyes opened wide. 'So Paul locked it?' She took the cushion from behind her head, and held it in both hands. 'Caterine's perfume,' she said. It reached Jenny faintly. 'She always used it. Paul can lock that door, but Caterine's everywhere still. Don't you feel that?'

She looked with dark intent eyes at Jenny. Jenny had not lived with Caterine for the last eight years, seeing her daily as Lorraine had done. Although while their mother lived no day had passed without Caterine's name being spoken. Jenny had always lived in Caterine's shadow, and she knew what Lorraine meant.

'She loved this house,' said Lorraine. 'When we were entertaining you could look around in here sometimes and everybody would be watching her, *everybody*. She glittered. Not just her clothes or jewels. Just – Caterine. And she's here still. She must still be here.'

Jenny sighed. She missed Caterine too, her beautiful glittering sister. Lorraine's little pillbox was on a table beside her and Lorraine opened it, tipped out a couple and swallowed them.

'I've got to get a good night's sleep,' she said as though Jenny had protested. 'Lying awake is dreadful. But I do feel better today, I really do, and I'm glad I went down to the shop.'

'Are you going again tomorrow?'

'Yes.'

Jenny said, 'I'm doing a couple of hours' office work in the morning.' She explained how that had come about and Lorraine said:

'Yes, of course, you were a secretary, weren't you? Somehow I've always thought of you as being at home, looking after your mother.'

'So I was, for years.'

'Yes.' Lorraine was apprehensive, anticipating further trouble. 'Jenny,' she said slowly, 'Paul isn't an easy man to work for. He doesn't make many allowances if things go wrong.'

You only had to look at Paul Tremain to know that, but Jenny said, 'Thanks for the warning, but I think I'll be working mostly for Mr. Morrison.'

'Well, he won't shout at you,' said Lorraine. 'Caterine used to say he wouldn't raise his voice if the house was on fire.'

Jenny laughed. She didn't point out, 'I may have been the stay-at-home sister, but I was among the bright ones at school. Paul shouldn't have to make too many allowances for me.' But that was what she was promising herself. . . .

Later, when Lorraine went to her room, Jenny walked along to the kitchen and it was like last night so far as Eb and Ebby were sitting there. But tonight Ebby said, 'Here's your chance. He's still in the office.'

Jenny's heart sank.

'So how about going in and telling him he's working too late?' said Ebby.

'Take no notice of her.' Eb was shocked at the suggestion. His wife must have been telling him what Jenny was saying this morning, and Jenny was stuck with it.

She said, 'He can sack me now, I'm on the payroll,' and before Eb or her own common sense could stop her she turned and went back again down the corridor into the hall, then drew a deep breath before tapping lightly on the office door.

Paul called, 'Yes?'

She opened the door. He was working, he had papers on the desk, and a pen in his hand. She began nervously, 'Er – could I—?' and he said:

'You could fetch some coffee.'

She sped to the kitchen and was back with a tray as fast as Ebby could perk it. Paul said absently, 'Thank you.' He drank his coffee still reading papers, making alterations and additions, while Jenny sat at Mr. Morrison's desk, cleared of everything but the typewriter, and sipped from the cup she had poured for herself.

Any minute Paul was going to ask, 'Why are you still here?' and she would say, 'It's half past ten, don't you ever stop working?' No, perhaps not. But she could say what time it was, and she could point out that it was late.

Paul said, 'There are pencils and a pad in the top right-hand drawer. Take a memo for Joe, will you?'

He rattled it off, but she got it down. 'Now read it back,' he said.

On her mettle, she read it back, with a growing little glow of achievement, typed it out very carefully and took it across to him. Then he said, 'It's time you called it a day, Jenny.'

'I came in here to tell you that.'

'Did you?' He smiled. 'And you're right. Good night.'

She said good night to him and wondered if he would go to bed now. As she passed Lorraine's door she hoped that Lorraine slept peacefully. Timmy slept. Jenny stepped with care over the model railway lines, silver in the moonlight like a spider's web, and looked down on him with love.

Through Caterine she was involved with them all. With Timmy ... with Lorraine ... With Paul, who carried Tremain and who must not break. ...

CHAPTER FOUR

AUGUST slipped by. Jenny earned her keep, and Mr. Morrison's approval, with a few hours' office work most mornings. He never said much, but he had a weakness for perfect pages of typing, particularly figures, and when he murmured 'Capital' Jenny always felt absurdly gratified.

Paul took perfect typing for granted, although he never missed a detail. Whether it was a cottage roof needing repair, or a mass of complicated data about farm or mining machinery, he needed no prompting; and when he came across thick-headedness or inefficiency he wasted no words.

He could be a swine, and Jenny spent a fair amount of time disliking him heartily. The rest of the time she veered between grudging respect and growing admiration, because he did the work of half a dozen men and he did it formidably well. He could be tough to callousness, but just when she was glowering with disapproval she would hear something like the story of Dolly's Andrew.

She was smarting on behalf of a maintenance man, who had not reported a piece of faulty equipment, when she went into the dining-room which Dolly was giving its weekly polish.

Andrew's A-level results had arrived recently and they were still a subject of rejoicing for Dolly. She told Jenny about them all over again – four, no less, and three of them merits – and Jenny said how lucky Dolly was in her son.

'It would have been a very different tale if Mr. Tremain hadn't stood by him,' Dolly said softly.

Andrew it seemed had run wild at fourteen after his father died, ending up a young tearaway in a Birmingham magistrates' court. Paul had got him a solicitor, stood bail, and made himself responsible for Andrew's future conduct, and Andrew had been given a second chance.

His mother chuckled, polishing the table until her smile showed in it. 'The magistrates didn't scare him,' she told Jenny, 'but by golly, Mr. Tremain did.

'He went back to school, and he daren't not work because Mr. Tremain wanted reports, and he's a clever boy and he'll make a good doctor. His heart's set on it now, but it could have been very different.'

Jenny returned to the office after that, the memory of Paul blasting the maintenance engineer merging into the picture of Paul handling a teenager whose whole life was in the balance. Andrew came up to Moidores to say goodbye before he set off for college. He was a nice lad, with more than a glint of humour, and he openly hero-worshipped Paul Tremain. . . .

There was an Indian summer this year. Jenny and Timothy swam most days while the school holidays lasted. After the first week they were joined by a swarm of Timmy's friends, and his sea fears seemed allayed. Perhaps for as long as the summer lasted.

Jenny tried horse-riding again. The horses were stabled at Blades, the home farm, and they were beautiful without exception. Even Snowy who was ageing and putting on weight, and although hardly as short or as wide as Jenny would have liked, was the steadiest of the lot.

She found them all endearing. She would have preferred petting and feeding them to sitting on them, but Timothy and Lorraine were patient with her and only took her across easy ground.

Lorraine was back at the shop now, but she usually rode once or twice a week. She was an accomplished horsewoman and Timothy rode well, and sometimes they would gallop ahead with the wind streaming through Lorraine's long fair hair and touselling Timmy's thick dark mop, while Jenny plodded on feeling like part of the herd heading for the old corral, knowing that at any sign of stampede they would be back to round her up in no time.

Fortunately Snowy was content to amble, and Jenny

refused to urge him on to anything else. Mastering the rhythm of the amble and the trot was enough for her.

During their rides she renewed old acquaintances at the farms on the Tremain estate. The same families were still there, but a grandmother had died at Blades, and at another farm the daughter had married and moved away.

Rolf's father still farmed his smallholding. It adjoined the home farm where the horses were stabled, they usually rode past it, but when Jenny asked, 'Shall we call on the Perries?' Lorraine hesitated as Timmy turned his chestnut pony through the open five-barred gate, galloping down the rough track that led to the grey-stone farmhouse and buildings.

The girls followed. Timmy had ridden round to the back of the house and when they caught up Mrs. Perrie was with him. Jenny remembered Rolf's mother laughing over the misadventure of the pigsty, producing a hot bath followed by a hot drink, and the whole thing being a riotous joke. But she looked much older now. Pale and very composed. It was hard to imagine her giggling.

She welcomed Jenny and said how pleased she was to see them all, and they must come in for a cup of tea. She brought out eggshell china and served the tea in the parlour, and they talked about the weather and the changes since Jenny was last here. Jenny hadn't noticed many, but Mrs. Perrie could think of a few.

They stayed for about half an hour, by which time Timothy was fretting to get on with their ride and Jenny was running out of small talk. Lorraine hadn't contributed much, although she didn't make the first move to go. It was Jenny who got up off her chair and said how nice it had been seeing Mrs. Perrie again.

'Call any time,' said Rolf's mother.

'Thank you,' said Jenny. 'Remember us to Mr. Perrie and Rolf. I'm sorry we missed them.'

'I will,' said Mrs. Perrie.

Lorraine said, 'Thank you' too, and Mrs. Perrie said graciously:

'You are more than welcome, Miss Tremain.'

Timmy held Snowy's head while Jenny mounted and Jenny grinned and said: 'Do you remember the pigsty? I'm not much better now,' and Mrs. Perrie laughed for a moment.

She wasn't looking much older, Jenny realized. It was her manner that gave that impression. There was a reserve about her now, a withdrawal. When she had just laughed that was the Mrs. Perrie Jenny remembered. Now she was grave again, waving them good-bye, turning to go back into the house before they had quite rounded the corner.

Timmy trotted ahead and when she was out of earshot Jenny said, 'She's changed.'

'Yes.'

'What's the matter with her?'

'Paul bosses Rolf about, I suppose, and his mother doesn't like it.'

'I shouldn't have thought Rolf would have whined at home about what happened at work.'

Lorraine shrugged. Jenny went on, 'And Paul doesn't pull rank unless things are going wrong.'

'Doesn't he?' Lorraine laughed harshly. 'He laid down the law for Caterine. And Rolf may be manager of that mine, but I don't suppose Paul lets him forget who owns it.'

She dug her heels into her horse's sides and galloped away, beyond Timothy, who thought she was racing and tried to keep up with her, then when she outstripped him came back to Jenny to ask, 'Where's Auntie Lorraine gone?'

'I don't know,' said Jenny. 'I think she felt like a ride on her own.'

No further mention was made of the Perries, but they didn't call in again. . . .

By the time Timothy and the other children went back to school after the holidays Jenny had a way of life going for her in Tremain. It had to be temporary, she knew that, but she was enjoying it while it lasted, working longer and well-paid hours in the office, giving Lorraine a hand in the shop sometimes.

Trade in the shop would be less during the winter months, of course, and then the artists stockpiled for next season or sent their work to the agents and the galleries. Jack Bastaple was working for an exhibition in London in the spring.

Jenny was seeing rather a lot of Jack. Not dates exactly, but when she went down to Tremain he usually materialized before long. He always looked into the shop when she was helping there, and she had had several bread and cheese lunches with him at the Tremain Arms.

Jenny was making more friends than she had ever had in her life. She found the artists congenial company, Grace Norbrook in particular, and her husband Ben, a sculptor who worked in basaltic rock and the greenish granite of Cornwall, fashioning rugged heads and powerful neo-lithic-like figures. And she had always liked the fishermen and the shopkeepers and the folk who ran the two pubs.

Sometimes she and Lorraine would stay down in Tremain for their evening meal, usually they ate with Grace, but it was always Jack who walked back with them to Moidores.

Timothy had had no more nightmares. With Ebby keeping a watchful guard Jenny felt fairly safe in being away from the house for a few hours. She would not have risked being away all night, nor away from him any time if there had been a threat of storm.

There had not, in the two months since she came, although now the Indian summer was drawing to a close and this Saturday the tourist trade was very much on the ebb.

Customers had been few, and Jenny stood at the window looking out. Timmy was at home, the quayside was almost deserted, and the boats bobbing on the water were regulars, natives. Paul Tremain's *Mylor* was at its usual anchorage in the mouth of the harbour.

Jenny had never been aboard. None of the family had so far as she knew, although Paul sailed most week-ends. Not today, though, it seemed. She had asked Mr. Morrison if he went along and he had said, 'I find sailing a very overrated pastime. I never go sailing.'

'Who does Paul take with him?' she'd asked, and expected to be told to ask Paul, because it was certainly no business of hers, but he'd said, 'Dan Blaskie occasionally.'

Dan was one of the few remaining fishermen in Tremain, the shoals were getting sparser, the fishing less profitable. 'Usually he sails alone,' said Mr. Morrison.

Timmy had told her that the first day she came here. It looked a beautiful boat, it seemed a shame Paul wouldn't share it. Jenny would have given her eye-teeth – well, nearly – to sail in it, but she knew she would never find the courage to ask outright.

She often looked at it wistfully. She did now, and Jack who was wandering around the shop asked, 'What's the sigh for?'

'The sun,' said Jenny promptly. 'The weather's breaking.' Clouds were sculling across the sky, and the sea looked dull and sullen. There was no one in the shop now, but Jenny and Jack, and Lorraine in the small office at the back going through some order books.

'Pity,' said Jack.

'You should be pleased,' Jenny teased. 'There'll be no one left in Tremain but the people who live here.'

Jack had come to stand beside her. He said:

'It's a different place then. Are you staying to see?'

Did Timothy still need her here? There had been no talk of her going, and although she was hardly irreplaceable in the office she knew that Mr. Morrison at least would prefer not to replace her.

Jack said, 'You might not like it in the winter, Jenny.'

'No?'

He looked out with her across the grey waters. 'When the people have gone,' he said, 'you'd find it very lonely.'

She almost gasped. It seemed crazy that the man who was her closest male friend in Tremain should know so little about her that he thought she would be lonely with-

73

out the press of people around. You could be lonely in cities, didn't he know that?

'I'll miss you,' he said, as though it was certain she would go soon, and she supposed it was.... 'Will you come to Tremain for a month or so?' Paul had asked at the beginning of August. They were into October now. Soon she must go home.

She must go home. She went out of the shop, crossing to the harbour wall. No one played on the shingle today, a man was caulking an upturned dinghy, seagulls wheeled overhead, and beyond the harbour low clouds smudged the outline of the Witch's Rock.

She saw every detail with singing joy, and knew that if she left here she would be sick with longing for it. The house in which she had lived all her life held no part of her. She was alive here, and strong, and no one was going to send her away. She was home.

Jack was holding her arm and saying, 'Don't go too soon, Jenny. We'll all miss you.'

Moidores was big enough for a regiment, no one needed Jenny's room. Paul would never ask her to go; Ebby had said she was part of the family. She couldn't announce, 'I've decided to stay for ever,' but she had, and she felt light-headed with happiness.

If Paul should turn me out of Moidores, she thought, I'll live in the cave in the Witch's Rock. And Jack believed she was smiling because he had told her he would miss her.

He said, 'You're very sweet, and you will come to my exhibition, won't you?'

Some of his pictures were stored in the shop, some in the studio. Jack lived in one of the cottages in the side streets, but he did most of his indoor work in the vast studio, with its high-beamed ceiling, over what had been the boatbuilder's shed. This room had plenty of light, and several of the artists used it. Jenny had been up there, the place was a bit like a clubroom, and she thought she had seen all the pictures Jack had ready for the exhibition so far.

He was working hard. They all said the exhibition

74

should be a success, in a first-class gallery, owned by a friend of Paul's who had a high reputation as an art critic. Jack Bastaple would be getting an international shop window for his work for a couple of weeks, and of course Jenny would go along to see the pictures on display.

'Of course,' she said.

As they went back into the shop she picked up a shell from the basket by the door and put it to her ear. The old trick of 'listening to the sea' never failed to fascinate her, it was just like a crooning song.

Lorraine had come out of the office and was tidying a shelf. Jack went to help her, and Jenny stayed where she was. There was really nothing to do, there would probably be no more customers today. The clouds seemed to thicken while she watched them and she thought – we could be in for a storm, perhaps I should be getting back to the house.

The shell was cool against her cheek, so perfectly shaded and patterned that if it had been man-made it would have been worth more than any of the sculptures they were producing. She turned it, wonderingly, and Jack queried, 'What's so marvellous about that one?'

'Look at it.' She held it in scooped hands, and he looked at her and said suddenly:

'Come and see a picture.'

'What picture?'

'One of mine, of course.'

'All right?' she asked Lorraine, who said:

'You don't have to ask me,' and went on with her shelf dressing.

They went out through the side door into the court-yard and Jenny headed for the steps up to the studio when Jack said, 'It isn't there. It's in the cottage.'

She followed him, he walked fast. His cottage was about three minutes away, in the narrow streets at the bottom of the hill, a little back from the sea. You stepped straight into a small cosy room, with a table and dresser, a couple of comfortably sagging armchairs, and three saddleback chairs. One door was closed, another opened into a kitchen.

Jack said, 'Not much of a place.'

'I like it,' said Jenny. She would have liked it. It was untidy, but a little caring could have made it charming.

'Compared with Moidores,' said Jack.

'Who's comparing it with Moidores?'

He laughed. 'Nobody, so far as I know. One of these days when I'm rich I'll buy my own castle. Sit down.'

She sat. He said, 'I want this hanging where it hits everyone who walks into that gallery, and no one has seen it yet.'

She should have been flattered, but somehow she was uneasy. 'Why should I be the first?'

He reached to touch her cheek. 'Because I don't want you shocked.'

'Shocked?'

This time he laughed at her. 'You don't need to blush. It isn't pornography. It couldn't be more restrained.'

'I'm not blushing.' She knew he would not produce a gimmicky shocker for his exhibition, so she asked intuitively, 'Is it Caterine?'

He sometimes did portraits. He had sketched Jenny once, over lunch at the Tremain Arms. 'Yes,' he said.

'But why hide it?'

He opened the second door and she heard him going up the stairs, his footsteps overhead. He brought the painting down with him.

The window in this room was small, with net curtains drawn across and short blue-sprigged curtains each side. They were a woman's curtains, perhaps his mother or a girl-friend had chosen them. Jenny looked at them, although she knew she must turn her head now and look at the picture.

The room was too dark to see a painting clearly, but she didn't want the light switched on. When she saw Caterine she might weep, and shadows would hide tears.

He put the canvas on the dresser, beside the bread board with a cut cottage loaf and a bread knife, drew the sprigged curtains across the window and flicked down the light switch, and Caterine looked at Jenny.

Jenny sat very still.

Caterine's hair fell loose. She wore a green scarf like foam on her shoulders, and ropes of pearls around her throat and in her hair. She held a shell, as Jenny had held that shell minutes ago; golden rings on every finger, and heavy gold bracelets that fettered her wrists. She was the sea witch, a prisoner, chained with jewelled fetters, and Jenny demanded hoarsely, 'What are you trying to do?'

She got up and went closer. It was Caterine. Everyone who had ever seen her would recognize her. The picture would be a talking point, and a savage indictment, because there was an anguish in the beautiful eyes as piercing as though the painting screamed.

Jack said heavily, 'Remind some of them that she didn't escape.'

'You can't do this! That's my sister, that's Timothy's mother. Caterine was not a prisoner.'

It was well painted. It would probably sell. It might even be printed. Caterine's death and the legend of the sea witch would be enough to get this into the popular press where even Timothy's small friends might see it. She said, 'Sell it to me.'

'I'm sorry.'

'You want to sell it, don't you?'

He looked at her with narrow eyes. 'That wasn't why I painted it.'

She knew that well enough. This was revenge for everything about Paul that Jack Bastaple resented. It was because the cottage was not much of a place compared with Moidores, because there were tourists on the quayside, because Paul Tremain was Tremain.

He said, 'After the exhibition I'll give it to you.'

'You're not going to show it!'

'Klopper doesn't censor, even if he is Tremain's friend. This is a good painting, he'll hang it.'

He must mean the man who owned the gallery. Jenny said shrilly, 'You are not putting Timothy's mother on show, looking as though she had no hope in life!'

'Jenny,' Jack Bastaple gestured appeal, 'don't get hys-

77

terical. That's why I'm showing it to you now so that you have time to see it alone and calmly. Jenny, she *was* a prisoner.'

Jenny retorted, 'Come to that, we're all prisoners.'

'Sure, I know that. But Caterine was a special person. Tremain had no right—'

'You have no right to do this! I won't let this happen. It would be monstrous. It's a travesty!'

He almost laughed again then. 'Tremain gave her those bracelets on her last birthday. They weren't chained like handcuffs, but they should have been. And the pearls. Have you seen the pearls? I remember the eyes too. This isn't a travesty.'

'You loved her?'

The question seemed to surprise him, but he said, 'I suppose I did.'

It wasn't surprising, all men seemed to be attracted to Caterine, although Paul was the only one she had loved. Jack Bastaple's devotion must have counted for nothing, she'd never mentioned him to Jenny. But it might have been the resemblance between the sisters that made him seek Jenny's company, and it explained his hate for Paul and this painting.

She said, 'I'm sorry.'

'For me? Because I must have loved her?'

'Because it's left you hating. Please, Jack, don't send this painting to London. Please let me have it.'

'I'm sorry.'

Nothing would change his mind. She saw in the stubborn set of his mouth that no matter who suffered – and the hurt would go further than Paul, certainly to Lorraine, almost certainly to Timothy – Jack Bastaple would have that picture of Caterine hanging in that London gallery.

Jack stood by the window. Jenny picked up the bread knife and slashed the picture. She had never in her life before wilfully destroyed anything. She had never held a knife like a dagger, and in tearing Caterine's face she felt physical pain in herself so that she moaned.

It was the last thing he had expected. He couldn't be-.

lieve it, even while he was watching. He could neither move nor speak, and Jenny put down the knife and looked at her hands as though she expected to see blood on them.

Then he muttered, 'You're mad!'

'I couldn't let you do that.'

But she was a quiet girl, a gentle girl. It was hard to believe she was Caterine's sister, except for that family likeness. It was mind-blowing that she should destroy his painting and that she was not hysterical.

She was calm, not even trembling. He took a couple of steps towards her, and she looked steadily at him. She was not afraid, and he had a sudden insane conviction that she was stronger than he was. That if he struck her with all his strength she still would not flinch.

That was nonsense, he could have killed her with a blow. He wanted to kill her, and he crashed down on the table with clenched fists, and a paralysing force that almost broke the bones in his hands, so that he stood with bowed head gasping, 'Get out while you can!'

Jenny walked past him.

'I shall paint it again,' he said.

She couldn't stop him. If he did that she could do nothing.

As she reached the door he said through clenched teeth, 'Who are you protecting at Moidores – the child or the man?'

She lifted the latch. 'Caterine's child.' If he had loved Caterine he might remember Timothy while he painted. Caterine would not want her son to see that anguish in her eyes.

'Caterine's man,' said Jack Bastaple savagely. 'Don't ever forget it.'

Jenny opened the door, heard faint thunder and began to run. The storm was coming and she had to get to Timothy.

The storm came slowly but inexorably. As she hurried up the cobblestoned hillside the sky grew heavier, clouds massing together like a black blanket, making the air so oppressive that there seemed no oxygen in it.

Jenny had cramp in her side and was labouring painfully for breath by the time she reached the cliff-top road, racing against the storm. The first heavy drops of rain were falling now, the thunder was nearer, the lightning brighter.

She turned towards Moidores, forcing herself to keep running. Past the spot where Caterine's car had skidded – the weather must have been like this, the storm just breaking – looking up towards the house and the turret window where Timothy had stood that day.

He wouldn't be there now, Ebby would see to that, but wherever he was he could be panicking and Jenny had to get to him.

She ran for the kitchen door, that was always unlocked during daytime, and by now the rain was a deluge. She hadn't bothered to put on her coat when she'd left the shop to see Jack's painting. She was in a pink sweater and a navy pleated skirt, and both were sticking to her. As she dashed into the kitchen Dolly gave a little protesting squeak as though she had seen a mouse, 'Goodness, you're soaked! Come to the fire.'

'Hello.' Jenny could hardly get the word out. 'Where's Timmy?'

'With his father.' Dolly was mending household linen. She sat at the table, stitching a pillowcase, and Jenny went across to the fire in the inglenook, realizing that she could hardly have been wetter if she had swum all the way back to Moidores.

Timmy would be all right if he was with Paul. As soon as Jenny had her breath back she'd go and change. For the moment she stood and steamed, and the rain literally dripped off her on to the red polished flagstones.

The storm was right overhead, the thunder rolling, the lightning flashing. Jenny said, awestruck. 'Just listen to it!' but Dolly's expression had the tranquillity of a woman born and bred in Tremain.

'Sea witch weather,' said Jenny. Dolly nodded, busy with her small neat darning.

'So they say.' She gave the windows a glance and through the driving rain saw the forked lightning, and admitted that this was a fairish storm. 'I don't know whether I'll be getting home tonight.'

No one would turn out in this if they had any choice at all. Lorraine would have to stay down in the harbour until it passed.

Jenny wondered if she would call on Jack's cottage then to see if Jenny was still there ... what Jack would say.... 'I painted a picture of Caterine and Jenny destroyed it.' He had said he would paint it again. He must have worked in secret, from memory, but it was no secret now because Jenny knew. And who could she tell, 'He's painting Caterine so that anyone who sees it will feel she's happier dead, and wonder if she wanted to die'?

Ebby came into the kitchen and did a double take. 'Didn't expect to see you for a while.' Then she smiled, 'His father's with him.' She knew why Jenny had run back and she had expected to see her. 'Couldn't you have borrowed a mackintosh?' she said.

From Jack? Hardly. Jenny's toes squelched in her shoes and she looked down apologetically at the damp she was spreading. 'Sorry, I'll get changed.'

'Before you do,' said Ebby, 'look in the drawing-room. Mr. Paul said when you came would you look in.'

Dolly bit off a thread. 'You ought to get out of those wet things.'

'Timmy's a bit bothered,' said Ebby. That fixed the priorities. Jenny took her dripping self straight to the drawing-room.

A good fire was burning in here too, and in here the curtains were drawn. Paul sat on a settee, his arm around Timothy, and a book on the child's knee. As Jenny opened the door they both turned. Then Timothy scrambled down so that the book fell, and Jenny went towards him.

He said, 'Father said you were all right.'

'Of course I'm all right.' He reached for her hand and she brought him back to the fire.

'Where's Auntie Lorraine?'

'Still in the shop. I got caught in the rain on my way home. She'll come home when it stops raining.'

Jenny stooped to pick up the book and looked up at Paul and he knew that she had run through the storm to reach Timothy.

'You're awful wet,' said Timothy.

'Mmm.' She smiled. 'You should have seen the mess I made on the kitchen floor! Ebby's not very pleased with me. I'm just going to get changed.'

Everything must be casual. Probably all his life Timothy would dislike storms, they would always have that link in his mind with Caterine's accident. But Jenny had just come along the cliff road in the storm and the sea had not reached for her. The rain had soaked her, but she was smiling, and safe as his father had promised him.

Timmy said, 'I'm glad you came home.'

'I'll be back in five minutes,' she promised. She didn't say, 'I'll always come home,' but she would, she would.

She left the man and the child, and went to her little room, towelled herself dry, and dressed quickly. As she passed Caterine's door anger burned in her again against Jack Bastaple, because Caterine had been happy. Everyone in this house had loved Caterine.

They loved her and mourned her. Lorraine still blamed herself for not taking Caterine's part against Paul. That painting of Caterine chained would be searing for Lorraine. She still talked about her own weakness and Jenny was still reassuring her that she was in no way to blame.

Paul carried his grief alone, he talked of Caterine to no one. But nearly three months after her death he kept the door of her room still locked.

Downstairs now Timmy was lying flat on his stomach in front of the fire, reading his book. Paul still sat on the settee, also with a book. A particularly heavy peal of thunder crashed overhead as Jenny opened the door, and Timmy looked up at his father.

Paul didn't seem to notice the child's wide eyes on him. He turned another page and Timmy turned back to his reading. Paul's presence was reassurance enough now, it seemed.

The thunder had drowned the lesser sound of the opening door, and Jenny stood watching them, holding the tray she had just brought from the kitchen. She would have been happier to see Timothy still held close. He wasn't really scared any more, but he was not beyond needing an arm around him.

She said, 'I took my things into the kitchen to dry and I brought some bread back to make some toast.' She had also brought plates, butter, strawberry jam, peanut butter, and cheese.

'Smashing!' grinned Timothy.

They made toast while the storm raged on. Behind those heavy curtains the lightning in sky and sea would be as spectacular as a giant firework display. It didn't get through the curtains, but the thunder rolled and rumbled.

While they were busying themselves Jenny talked to Timmy who was soon nattering away nineteen to the dozen. He toasted the bread and she spread it thick with butter, and when they had a tottering pile Paul asked, 'When do we eat it?'

'We have done a lot.' Timmy turned a glowing face from the fire to survey their handiwork. 'Good job we're hungry.'

Jenny asked Paul gravely, 'Plain or à la carte?'

'Jam and peanut butter's nice.' Timothy spoke like a connoisseur and Paul said hastily:

'Cheese.'

'Jam and peanut butter sounds delicious,' said Jenny.

'Are you having it?' they both asked.

'Why not?'

'What it is to be young!' sighed Paul, and Jenny said gaily:

'Don't be pompous!' then wondered if she had gone too far, but Paul laughed and Timothy said:

'Shall I spread it for you?'

'I'll spread my own,' she said. 'We all will.'

By scraping hers very thin it wasn't too dreadful. They could sit quieter now, there was no need to keep talking. The thunder was no longer overhead and Timmy was relaxed and a little sleepy from the warmth of the fire. He sat, leaning against Jenny, and they found pictures in the fire.

Paul went on reading his book, and half an hour later when Lorraine came in Jenny and Timmy were into an involved tale of outer space. The fire was the planet Mars and they had reached the stage where they were happily watching a cartoon show.

Timmy invited, 'Come and look, Auntie Lorraine,' while Lorraine knelt down beside them and swore she could see the three-headed monster who immediately dissolved into a shower of sparks.

'They keep doing that,' Timmy confided. 'It's their secret weapon.'

'Wheee!' said Lorraine. She had been worried about Timothy, although she had known that Dolly and Ebby would do everything they could to keep him from panicking. She hadn't known where Paul was, she had hoped that Jenny had got home.

A couple of customers had come in after Jenny went off with Jack, and by the time Lorraine finished serving them the rain was deluging down.

She grinned at Jenny over Timmy's head. 'Did Jack bring you home?'

'No.'

She deduced that Jenny had run like mad, and loved her for it. She asked, 'What was the picture like?'

'A – seascape,' said Jenny.

'Good?'

'I don't know. I didn't like it much.'

'I hope you didn't say you didn't like it. Jack Bastaple always takes criticism badly. He's touchy about his work.'

'Hard luck!' snapped Jenny.

Lorraine let it go. But later, after dinner, when Lorraine and Jenny were back in this room alone, she took it up again and asked, 'What did you say to Jack about his painting?'

Jenny almost told her. But there was something so vulnerable about Lorraine and this was an ugly thing. Lorraine wouldn't understand how Jack could have painted

84

that picture, nor how Jenny could have destroyed it.

Remembering brought an acrid taste to Jenny's mouth. She wasn't proud of what she had done, it would be hard to justify. Perhaps he wouldn't paint the picture again. When he did — if he did — would be time enough for Lorraine to know.

Jenny said quietly, 'I said I didn't like it.'

'Oh dear!' Lorraine winced. 'I'd have thought you'd have had more sense than that. They're all touchy about their work, but Jack needs handling with kid gloves.'

Jenny bit hard on her lip. This was black comedy if Lorraine only knew, and it got worse.

'You do like Jack, don't you?' Lorraine sounded concerned. 'I know he likes you.' ... Until today. Today he had bruised his hands to keep them from striking her. ... 'He always asks if you're coming down to the shop.'

Jenny said, 'I don't think he'll be asking again,' and Lorraine, who had been in a mood of gentle raillery until now, caught a deadly serious note.

She stopped smiling. 'Not over a painting? Oh, for goodness' sake make it up, you idiot! That's stupid!'

Jenny said nothing, but from her expression Lorraine knew she was on dangerous ground. There must have been far more than tactlessness on Jenny's part and huffiness on Jack's. Perhaps Jack had made a pass — although Lorraine would have thought Jenny could have cooled that situation if she'd wanted it cooled.

They had left the shop friends, and for weeks now Lorraine had been watching their friendship approvingly. She liked Jack, he was a good painter and he was nice, and he and Jenny had looked right together. But something had finished their friendship that Jenny was not going to talk about. 'I don't think we'll make it up,' said Jenny.

Lorraine picked at the brocaded arm of her chair with a fingernail, raising several threads of the pattern. As she tried to pat them down again she asked, 'Jenny, have you ever been in love?'

'I haven't had much chance. Mind you, there was this fantastic chap at the swimming pool. Only it was my butterfly stroke that turned him on, not me. He was the swimming coach.' Lorraine laughed, but almost at once Jenny regretted having answered flippantly. She hadn't been in love. She hadn't had much chance. But it had been a serious question and she asked, 'Have you?'

Lorraine went on smoothing the brocade, her long hair veiling her face. 'No. One or two false alarms, but no. Caterine said we should be two old maids, you and I, did you know that?'

'Yes.' She had said it to Jenny too, teasing in loving fashion. 'There's a long way to go before then,' said Jenny.

'But how do you know when you're really in love?'

There hadn't even been any false alarms in Jenny's life. She was younger and less experienced than Lorraine and yet she felt immeasurably more mature. She thought – I'll know.

But she said nothing and after a moment or two Lorraine jumped up and crossed to the windows. She pulled the curtains apart and said, 'The air's still heavy. The storm's still around.'

It growled like tigers in the distance, and Jenny went upstairs several times to check on Timmy, but he was always asleep.

It was almost too hot for comfort. When she went to bed Jenny had to leave the windows closed and the curtains drawn, but she kept the doors open between the rooms and into the corridor.

After one crash of thunder Timmy gave a faint cry and she was out of bed in a flash. He stirred and raised his head and she said, 'It's all right, Timmy, go to sleep.' He looked such a little boy, curled beneath the counterpane. 'Hush, close your eyes now, shhh!'

She began to croon to him, humming very softly, hardly a tune, just something to lull him to sleep, and he snuggled down again and his eyes closed.

She went back to her own bed, and when the next thunder crash came Timmy didn't whimper, he called sleepily, 'Auntie Jen – sing a bit,' so she went on with her tuneless tune until she sang both Timmy and herself to sleep. . . .

86

The summer was over next day. The storm had left everything grey. The sky and the sea merged, and the moors were drab with mud. There was no riding today, and there would be few holidaymakers in Tremain.

After breakfast Jenny went into the office. She wasn't working, it was Sunday; she was typing a letter of her own to Louie Sumner, back in the house that Jenny owned but that had never been her home.

When the phone that was a direct line from the mine rang she answered it. 'Who's that?' said a man's voice.

'Jenny Douglas. You want Mr. Tremain? I'll get him for you.'

The man said, 'Tell him there's been a rock fall in Branch Three, and Rolf Perrie's trapped.'

Paul was in the morning-room reading newspapers, she knew that. She ran to tell him, and he got up without a word and strode fast for the office.

'Not Rolf?' Jenny turned and it was Lorraine. She wouldn't have recognized the voice. She would hardly have recognized the face, which was chalk white. 'Oh, please, Jenny – not Rolf. . . .'

And Jenny knew then for sure that Rolf Perrie mattered a great deal to Lorraine.

CHAPTER FIVE

'WHAT did they say? What's happened?' Lorraine clutched Jenny's arm so hard that it hurt.

'That there'd been a rockfall,' Jenny repeated.

'And Rolf?'

The man on the phone from the mine had said, 'Rolf Perrie's trapped.' Trapped could mean anything, it could mean crushed and buried alive, and Jenny wished now that she hadn't mentioned Rolf's name. But she had given Paul the message parrot fashion.

She said, 'Just that Rolf was there,' and Lorraine swayed, face in her hands. Jenny got her into a chair and remembered how she had felt herself when the news came about Caterine.

When Lorraine whispered 'No,' Jenny recalled that reaction that if you denied it hard enough it wouldn't have happened.

She stood useless, and after a few moments Lorraine took her hands from her face, then looked at Jenny and said, 'He's got to be all right.' Jenny nodded. 'Where's Paul?' whispered Lorraine. Jenny gestured towards the door. The shock of hearing Rolf's name must have dazed Lorraine so that she hadn't seen Paul leave the room, but she jumped up now and ran into the hall as Paul was coming out of the office.

She half screamed, '*Paul!*' and he came across to them. 'What's happening?'

Lorraine was ashen, but Paul looked calm and sounded calm. He said, 'Perrie was in one of the branch tunnels examining the working face, and there's been a fall at the entrance to the tunnel. We'll soon have it cleared.'

'How do you know it's only at the entrance? How do you know the whole tunnel hasn't caved in?'

He explained, 'Because the phone link is still intact. They've spoken to him.'

'He's *alive*?' She sounded as though she daren't believe

it, and Paul turned to go, saying:

'I'll ring you as soon as there's any more news.'

'I'm coming.'

'No.' His tone was flatly final. 'You stay here. Jenny,' he looked at Jenny for the first time, 'give her a couple of tranquillizers and then stay by the phone. There might be calls coming through.'

Then he went, wasting no more time. Lorraine said huskily, 'I've got to see for myself. Paul might have been lying to me.'

'Why on earth should he lie?'

'You don't understand,' said Lorraine darkly. 'Will you come?' And Jenny thought – maybe I'm beginning to understand.

Lorraine had a car. Jenny couldn't keep her here against her will if she was determined to drive to the mine, and this time she seemed to be making her own decision in defiance of Paul. She was going, and she was in no state to go alone.

'Wait while I ask Eb or Ebby to listen to the phone,' said Jenny, and ran to find the Ebsworths. She found Ebby, bustling around in the kitchen, and asked, 'Where's Timmy?'

'In the greenhouse with Eb. Do you want him?'

Jenny didn't want to say this in front of Timothy, that was all. She said breathlessly, 'There's been a rockfall at the mine. Rolf Perrie's involved and Lorraine's determined to go and see what's happening.

'They've just phoned to tell Paul and he said Lorraine was to stay here and I was to sit by the phone. But she's not going to stay and somebody will have to go with her if she's driving, so would you or Eb listen for the phone?'

Ebby looked worried. 'If Mr. Paul told you to wait you'd better.'

'Tell Lorraine that,' said Jenny.

'Bad, is it?' asked Ebby.

'I took the call. He said a rockfall and Rolf Perrie was trapped and tell Paul.'

'Oh dear!' Ebby sighed, and they hurried.

Lorraine was standing in the open door of the office looking at the silent telephone as though she was hypnotized by it. She was obviously dreading it ringing, convinced there would be no good news, and Ebby said gently, 'You can't do any good down there, chicken, only get in the way.'

Jenny had never heard Lorraine called chicken before, and Lorraine half smiled. The endearment brought memories of long-ago reassurances and comfort: Ebby bathing a cut knee, fussing away a childish fear. 'I won't get in the way,' Lorraine spoke tremulously, 'but I have to be there.'

Ebby didn't argue. She gave Lorraine a quick hug. 'And I'll say a little prayer.'

'Yes, Ebby, pray for him,' whispered Lorraine. 'Are you coming, Jenny?'

Paul had left, of course. If he hadn't he would have stopped her because she shouldn't have been handling a car. She was shaking so that she could hardly turn the ignition key, and when she did Jenny stretched across and turned it off again.

This was brutal but necessary. 'Listen to me,' said Jenny, 'Caterine drove too fast when she shouldn't have been driving at all. If we're going to the mine we're going slowly.'

'Caterine – now Rolf!' Lorraine wasn't weeping, but the black horror was back in her eyes and Jenny said with deliberate calm:

'Paul told you that Rolf was talking on the phone and that they'd soon get him out.'

'I'll believe that when I see him.'

'Does Paul lie?'

'No,' Lorraine admitted.

'All right, then. Now drive sensibly or I'll stop the car – I do know which is the handbrake; and if you want to get there you'll have to walk.'

Jenny would have preferred to walk, although it was some distance and a miserably grey day, but Lorraine pulled herself together with an obvious effort. The bullying seemed to be working, although if it came to a tussle there was no guarantee at all that Jenny would be able to stop the car.

They turned left from Moidores heading along the cliff road away from Tremain, then turning right for nearly two miles over the old road that had been cleared and resurfaced when Paul Tremain opened the mine again ten years ago.

Lorraine drove steadily. Other cars passed them, but she kept her own speed doggedly down. The wide track, lined most of the way with spiky bushes, ran through rocky gorse-covered heathland over which sheep roamed. They had to brake a couple of times to avoid the moronic creatures, but neither girl spoke until, without warning, tears began to roll down Lorraine's cheeks and Jenny said softly, 'Pull in, love.'

Then Lorraine stopped the car and put her head on folded arms on the steering wheel, and Jenny slipped an arm around her promising, 'It will be all right,' hoping and praying that it would; while Lorraine hiccuped, 'It's – Purdie's Beck. I'm sorry, I'm making a fool of myself.'

The beck was a stream some distance from the track, bubbling between high boulders, and Lorraine looked across at the boulders, her lips quivering and her voice unsteady. 'We used to meet there. We used to ride and meet each other there.'

So it wasn't that Lorraine had suddenly realized how fond she was of Rolf. There had been a time when they had had a meeting place.

She was talking to herself rather than to Jenny. 'The way I feel now I must have been in love with him.'

But when Jenny had asked if Rolf was in any way special in her life Lorraine had said, 'Rolf Perrie? Good heavens, *no*!' Jenny had thought then that the denial was over-emphatic. Several things were making more sense now.

Lorraine said, 'Paul said it was infatuation,' and that made Jenny gasp.

'What had it got to do with Paul?'

'He'd have dismissed Rolf if we had got married.'

Jenny sagged back in her seat in appalled astonishment,

'Paul threatened to *sack* him?'

'More or less. And Rolf had just been made manager and there aren't that many mines, are there? He'd have had to emigrate.'

'*Why?*'

Lorraine's face was still wet with tears. She mouthed the words in bitter mockery. 'Because he didn't consider it would be a suitable match. He didn't think that Rolf would be able to keep me in the standard to which I am accustomed.'

That was very likely. Although who did the Tremains think they were? Why shouldn't Lorraine be a working man's wife?

Jenny's expression must have mirrored her thoughts, because Lorraine flushed and looked down at her own white hands on the steering wheel and said, 'I couldn't see Rolf victimized, could I? and I wasn't really sure then.'

She looked out of the window again at Purdie's Beck and said sadly, 'But if Paul had left us alone I know now that it would have been Rolf. I never wanted anyone else.'

Jenny said tartly, 'The others were eligible, I suppose? They came up to Paul's standards?'

The flush was fading from Lorraine's cheeks, she looked pale and lonely. 'Oh yes, very eligible. Except that I didn't want them.'

Jenny was sorry for her. Although whether her feelings for Rolf were deep, or whether hearing he was in danger had exaggerated them, there was no telling. She seemed to have accepted the break-up equably enough until now. But she hadn't replaced Rolf, and when Jenny asked, 'Has Rolf found anyone else?' she said, 'No,' with such certainty that she must have kept tabs on him.

'Do you want to go on?' said Jenny.

'Yes, I'm all right now.'

They drove past the old mine entrance. They had ridden this way before, and to Purdie's Beck, circling the buildings of the present-day minehead before they.

turned for home. And Lorraine had never said one single word about Rolf Perrie.

The old entrance was almost hidden by boulders. A thick beam of wood blocked the way in and a Danger notice marked it. But for the beam and the warning it would have been possible to walk straight into the wood-lined mouth of the shaft.

The wood was rotten and crumbling, some of it hundreds of years old. Attempts had been made over a century ago to replace the edging with cut stone, but the work had not been completed. The mine had fallen into disuse, and for generations of Tremains it had been simply a ruin, a bit of history.

But Paul Tremain had nothing unproductive on his estate. The price of metals was rising again, sky-high this time. The old tin mine, with rich untapped lodes awaiting excavation, was next best thing to a goldmine; and with all that going for the Tremains Paul could surely have afforded to let Lorraine choose a man who had intelligence and kindness, without acting as though a bank balance was the be-all and end-all.

A dank moist smell hung over the old mine entrance, but another quarter mile of new road and the picture was very different. Here the buildings were modern stores and offices. Narrow gauge rail tracks for the iron trucks wound out of the mine and curved round the site huts to a huge mound of gleaming clay and stone deposit, and cables led from the generator hut into the entrance of the mine.

Usually, even above ground, the place hummed with activity, but there would have been no mining here today. The workers would have been maintenance men. And Rolf. There had been no mention of anyone trapped but Rolf.

There was a small crowd of men. An ambulance and a fire service truck stood at the side, and a lorry with a truck beyond it was drawn up near to the entrance.

Cars half filled the parking lot, and Lorraine turned in her car to join them, parking it as far as she could from Paul's. As Jenny began to get out she said, 'Don't let Paul see you.'

Jenny swung round. 'See me? What about you?'

Lorraine didn't move. 'Jenny—' she hesitated, then said in a little rush, 'Please, Jenny, go and ask for me. I can't.'

Oh lor', thought Jenny, I wish I could drive. I wish I could have given Lorraine those tranquillizers. She said, 'All right,' and left Lorraine holding the steering wheel very tight and watching Jenny's retreating figure with wide frightened eyes.

Jenny picked her way towards the approach to the mine, over a morass of muddy clay, well trampled and wet with the leaking of water pipes and hoses leading to the mine. When she heard her name she looked around and spotted Mr. Morrison in the doorway of the office block.

She crossed to him. He wore a faint expression of disapproval, and as an extra mark of no welcome said nothing whatever to her but went into the office, presuming, quite rightly, that she would follow.

The general office had a lot of clerical equipment and a man sitting at a switchboard. There was no one else about. A door to a glass-partitioned section read, 'A. Rogan, Assistant Manager,' and an open door into another room, 'R. Perrie, Manager.'

Mr. Morrison had just gone through Rolf Perrie's door, and Jenny continued to follow. He closed the door as soon as she was in the room and said severely, 'Why did you not stay at Moidores? I presume you have Miss Tremain in the car?'

'Yes, she's in the car. What's happening?'

'There's been a rockfall.'

'I know, I took the message. What about Rolf?'

'He sounds in good spirits. Mr. Tremain told me to phone and tell you that all was under control. I spoke to Mrs. Ebsworth who was glad to hear it. And now perhaps you'll both go home again.'

Jenny pleaded, 'Will you come and tell Lorraine that it's all right?' He nodded and she led the way back to the car park and the car. She got into the seat by Lorraine as

Mr. Morrison was getting into the back seat, and she had to reassure Lorraine right away. From the looks of Lorraine every second counted, so Jenny said at once, 'Rolf isn't hurt. He's been talking to them.'

Lorraine turned to face Mr. Morrison, her voice a croak. 'How did it happen?'

He gave a crisp summary. 'Mr. Perrie was inspecting a working face when a truck came adrift on the slope, dislodging a pit prop. Some of the roof came down. They're clearing it now.'

He sounded as though this was no more than a tidying-up operation, but a runaway iron truck and a roof crashing down on you in an underground mine was horrific. And when part of a roof fell could there be a chain reaction?

Lorraine echoed Jenny's fears. 'What if there's another fall?'

'What would happen to Mr. Perrie, you mean?' His tone was dry. 'He has been instructed over the phone to get back. As the rubble is being removed the roof is being shored up, but the men who could be hurt are the team who are doing the clearing, not Mr. Perrie.'

'Oh.' Lorraine sighed with relief. Right now she only had thoughts for Rolf.

Mr. Morrison went on in the same dry voice, 'As it will be several hours before the rubble is cleared I do advise you both to go home.'

'Soon,' said Lorraine. 'I think I'd better wait a little. If Jenny doesn't mind.'

Jenny was still turned towards Mr. Morrison. She asked suddenly, 'Where's Paul?'

'Down there.'

Lorraine jerked round again. 'You mean getting the rubble out?'

'Of course that's what he means.' Jenny surprised herself, she sounded so snappish, but Lorraine didn't seem to notice. Lorraine said:

'Yes, that's where Paul would be,' and almost smiled. 'Well, he'll be all right, he's indestructible.'

'Is he?' Now Jenny sounded savage. 'You could bury

him alive and come back for him in six months' time, I suppose,' and Lorraine stared at her as Mr. Morrison chuckled.

'I would not advise it,' said Mr. Morrison. 'He might well dig himself out, and he would come up in a very ugly frame of mind.'

Jenny grinned, 'He would, wouldn't he?'

'If you stay near the car,' Mr. Morrison offered, 'I will keep you posted on progress.'

'Thank you,' said Jenny.

They watched him go. Lorraine said, 'I didn't mean I'm not worried about Paul, but he will be taking care, won't he? They do know the risks. They'll be watching for trouble.'

'I certainly hope so,' said Jenny.

The time was half past ten. It took six hours to get Rolf Perrie out of the mine. A dozen men worked at clearing, another eight at shoring up the roof and loading the rubble on to the trucks, which were hauled to the surface by the winching truck attached to the back of the lorry at the mine entrance.

Some of the time the girls sat in the car, sometimes they walked around, getting in no one's way, staying in the background, and Mr. Morrison kept his promise to keep them posted.

He reported the first small hole made through the barrier. Lack of air had been a hazard, he said – they hadn't thought of that – but it was all right now. And he came across to the car park to tell them when the stretcher was taken in.

'Stretcher?' Lorraine shrilled. 'Why can't he walk?' She was out of the car, past Mr. Morrison, making for the group at the mine entrance, and Jenny squirmed out of the passenger seat and ran to stop her.

'Wait a bit,' Jenny begged, so Lorraine waited until Mr. Morrison reached them, sounding testy.

'Miss Tremain, I beg of you, don't make a scene.' Lorraine did look capable of flinging herself down beside the stretcher. That, Jenny reflected, would not please Paul, and it might not please Rolf either. Rolf might find it very embarrassing.

Lorraine snapped, 'Of course I'm not going to make a scene!' and when Jenny loosed her arm she still walked fast, but she wasn't running now and she did hold back from the group.

Rolf didn't look too bad as they carried him out, and when he saw Lorraine he gave her a reassuring wave. She smiled and waved back, and while the stretcher was being lifted into the ambulance they went on smiling at each other.

There were a lot of men milling around, most of them wearing protective helmets and looking filthy, and when a hand fell on her shoulder for a split second Jenny didn't recognize Paul. Then he demanded, 'What are you doing here?' and she gulped and said:

'Just going.'

The ambulance was away. She grabbed Lorraine again and they went back to the car park.

They drove in silence. Whatever Lorraine's thoughts were now she wasn't sharing them. But when the car was in the garage and switched off she said, 'Thank you.'

'What for?'

'For coming with me. For listening to me.'

'What happens now?'

Lorraine's lips curved as they had done when she smiled at Rolf. 'He looked for me,' she said.

'I think he did.' Jenny grimaced. 'Paul did too.'

'Yes, I know.' And Jenny was dismayed to see how completely the happiness drained from Lorraine's face, and the look of apprehension that replaced it. . . .

Paul, Mr. Morrison and Anthony Rogan, the assistant manager of the mine, arrived at Moidores a couple of hours after the girls. Rolf had escaped with several broken bones in his foot. He had been X-rayed, put in plaster, and taken on his own insistence back to his parents' farmhouse. He had been lucky.

Mr. Morrison gave this information to the household, who were all sitting in the kitchen where Ebby had put on a huge tea. Paul had not looked in the kitchen. He had gone to change and would then be in the office.

'Sandwiches and coffee?' said Ebby.

'Capital,' said Mr. Morrison. 'We shall be working for most of the evening on reallocation of shift quotas.'

'That sounds like fun.' Lorraine's eyes danced mischievously; the good news about Rolf had put stars in them. The assistant manager grinned, but no one else did.

'Do you need a secretary?' Jenny asked, and Mr. Morrison said:

'Tomorrow morning, probably, but tonight I don't think so,' his meaning clear to everyone but Timmy and the assistant manager. Tonight Jenny would do well to keep out of Paul's way.

Later, when Timothy was in bed, and Lorraine said, 'I'm going down to the harbour,' that seemed a good idea. It would have been pleasant to spend the rest of the evening with Grace and the others, except for the prospect of facing Jack Bastaple again.

Keep out of Paul's way up in the house, keep out of Jack's way down in the harbour. . . . If Jenny went on like this the only safe place left for her soon would be the Witch's Rock.

'Coming?' said Lorraine.

'No.'

'Why not?'

'Because I don't want to see Jack again for a day or two.'

'You needn't,' said Lorraine gaily. 'We'll dodge him.'

There was room enough in Tremain to avoid a meeting, and putting it off wouldn't really help. What guarantee was there that Jack would feel any better in a day or two about having had his picture ruined? He'd have had more time to brood about it. He could well be angrier, if that was possible; and she couldn't dodge him for ever.

She said, 'I'll tell Ebby. She'll listen for Timmy.'

It was dark and damp outside although the lights of Tremain glowed warmly in the sky over the next cove. Lorraine's torch guided their footsteps until their eyes were accustomed to the night, by which time they were nearing the turning for Tremain. The track leading over the moors to the home farm was almost opposite and Lorraine stopped and said, 'Don't be mad at me, Jenny.'

Jenny knew what was coming, and she stormed, 'Why couldn't you say we were going to see Rolf? Why tell me all that nonsense about going down to the harbour?'

Lorraine said in a small voice, 'If you'd told Ebby she'd have told Paul.'

Jenny was exasperated. 'Stop acting like a child! If you want Rolf and he wants you it has nothing to do with anyone else, and I do not believe for one moment that Paul would sack him.'

'It isn't that easy.' Lorraine's long fair hair and pale face shimmered in the darkness, making her look waiflike, ghostlike. 'Rolf works for Paul and Mr. Perrie farms Paul's land, and Paul made it very clear that he didn't want our friendship to go beyond friendship.

'You might not believe that Paul would hurt the Perries – well, I'm not so sure, and I've known my brother a great deal longer than you have.

'But Rolf could have been killed today, and he's my friend and I want to talk to him. Are you coming with me or going down to the harbour or going back home?'

Jenny sighed, feeling trapped. The Perries' small-holding was next to the home farm, a twenty-minute walk by this lonely track across the moors. Not an inviting prospect, but Jenny was Lorraine's alibi. Jenny had told Ebby – and because she believed it she had been convincing – that they were going down to Tremain. So long as they returned together, and unless they were spotted in the wrong place, no one was going to question that. If they didn't return together the truth would out.

'Why can't you wait till tomorrow?' Jenny demanded.

'I want to see him now,' said Lorraine, mild but stubborn.

'But he's almost certainly got to rest. He's had a grim day, do you think he'll want to entertain visitors?'

'I think he'll want to see me,' said Lorraine softly. She began to walk away down the track and Jenny stood for a

99

moment. It was lonely and dark and not a walk for a girl alone. Jenny had to follow and when she caught up Lorraine said, 'Thank you.'

'Don't thank me,' said Jenny huffily. 'I feel an absolute fool playing cloak and dagger like this. What do we do if the house is full of his workmates?'

'I don't go in.' Lorraine slipped a hand through Jenny's arm. 'Jenny dear, don't be angry, I never had anyone to talk about Rolf with before. I am grateful.'

'Didn't you talk to Caterine?'

'Caterine laughed at me.'

Caterine laughed at most folk, but Lorraine was a sensitive girl, unsure of herself in spite of her looks and her position. Jenny said, 'She laughed at me too.'

'She called him my ploughboy.' But Rolf wasn't even a farmer, he was a highly qualified mining engineer. 'I'm sure she didn't mean it unkindly,' said Jenny, and Lorraine agreed quickly:

'No, she didn't, it was just her joke, she never took it seriously at all. Not many people knew, although it wasn't a secret. We'd known each other all our lives, of course, and when he came back from college and started work at the mine we went out together a few times, and we used to ride together.

'Then the manager retired and Paul made Rolf manager. Rolf was going to ask me to marry him, I know.'

The track beneath their feet was damp and clogging from the storm, and a bleak wind blew. Jenny pulled her coat tighter around her, holding it together at her throat.

'Only Paul stopped him,' said Lorraine. 'It's c-cold, isn't it?' and her teeth were chattering.

'Yes,' said Jenny. 'Very cold. Let's try to walk quicker.'

There were no cars in front of the Perries' farmhouse nor in the yard. All the same Lorraine hung back and said, 'Will you knock?'

Mr. Perrie answered the door. Jenny hadn't seen him since she came to Tremain this time, although she recognized him at once.

He still looked like an older edition of Rolf, but broader, perhaps more rugged. He knew her. 'Jenny Douglas.'

'Yes.' He saw Lorraine behind her and said:

'Come in, then,' so they stepped inside and he led the way into a room where Mrs. Perrie was sitting in a chair by the fire. Her face still showed the strain of the day, and she looked at Jenny and Lorraine for a moment as though they were enemies. Then she said:

'You were at the mine,' as if that was in their favour. 'Bill saw you.'

They hadn't noticed Mr. Perrie. Until Rolf was brought out they had been some distance from the entrance and the groups of men around it. But two girls would have been conspicuous. 'They wouldn't let me go,' said Mrs. Perrie.

Her husband patted her shoulder. 'You were better here, I know you.' He smiled at the girls. 'As it was she'd turned out all the cupboards and washed all the china and dropped half a dinner set before we got home.'

Jenny smiled too, any joke was welcome, but Lorraine was in no mood for smiling. 'How is Rolf?' She was nearly in tears, and Rolf's mother said:

'It's just his foot,' her voice trembling like Lorraine's, 'but he could have been killed.'

Lorraine went to Mrs. Perrie. 'How badly is he hurt?'

'They've set the bones,' his father sounded cheerful. 'There shouldn't be any complications. He's got to lie up for a week, and after that he can start getting about again.'

'It could have been—' Lorraine shuddered and closed her eyes.

'It could—' echoed Rolf's mother, and the two women gripped each other's hands, reliving their ordeal of waiting.

'But it wasn't,' Mr. Perrie reminded them.

'Can I see him?' Lorraine asked, and his mother said:

'He's supposed to be resting, but a minute or two can't

hurt, can it? Can it, Bill?'

Now Mr. Perrie looked serious. 'If Rolf's asleep,' he said, 'I don't think we ought to disturb him again tonight. I'll see if he is.'

'I will,' said Mrs. Perrie promptly. Lorraine went with her and Jenny felt that Mr. Perrie would rather she hadn't. He said slowly:

'Go on up, Miss Douglas.'

'I'll come again,' she said. If Rolf and Lorraine did have anything to say to each other they wouldn't want Jenny around.

'Take a chair, then.' Mr. Perrie's cheerfulness had quite gone. He sounded as though his thoughts were heavy and when Mrs. Perrie came back into the room she said:

'She's only staying a minute, Bill,' and looked at Jenny. 'He doesn't know she's here, I suppose?'

'Paul? No.'

'You've heard all about it, then?'

Mr. Perrie protested, 'I'm sure Miss Douglas—'

'Who told you?' asked Mrs. Perrie. 'Not Tremain, I'll be bound.'

'Lorraine,' said Jenny.

Mrs. Perrie went back to her chair by the fire. 'Our boy's not good enough for his sister.' She poked the fire, clattering the poker between the bars so energetically that her husband's protests were almost drowned. Then she looked up at him challengingly. 'That was what he said, wasn't it?'

Bill Perrie was not a young man. Waiting at the mine-head had been as harrowing for him as it had for his wife, here with friends and neighbours around her. He had watched the rescue operation, so far as a man could who was above ground, and he knew what part Paul Tremain had played. Right now he did not feel like disparaging Tremain or listening to his wife's tirade.

In the pocket of his tweed jacket he felt the reassuring shape of his pipe and said wearily, 'That's all in the past, all forgotten. Let's drop it, shall we?' Then he went out and lit his pipe and walked for a while around his farm buildings, getting some solace from a quiet smoke.

That business with Lorraine Tremain had been a rum do. Rolf had never talked much about it and his father had never worked out the rights and the wrongs of it. But Bill Perrie would have been happier tonight if he could honestly have believed it was all in the past and forgotten.

Sarah Perrie had no doubts who was in the wrong. When her husband had declined to discuss it she had turned back to Jenny, who sat uncomfortably unsure whether she was about to be confided in, or abused as a near-Tremain.

'His father was a very different sort,' said Mrs. Perrie nostalgically. Paul's father? Jack Bastaple had said that once. Mrs. Perrie pointed at Jenny. 'He'd sit in that chair you're in and take a glass of ale. Always had all the time in the world for a joke and a chat.'

That didn't sound much like Paul.

'He wouldn't have told Rolf he wasn't good enough,' said Sarah Perrie, and her hurt was for her son. She spoke with dignity, and the anguish of someone who would never forget.

That didn't sound like Paul either. It must have happened, but Jenny couldn't believe it. To Jenny it didn't ring true.

'It's not Lorraine's fault.' Lorraine was back in Mrs. Perrie's favour. 'She's a good girl, but she's no match for Tremain.'

Jenny wondered, 'Why didn't Rolf walk out? How could he go on working for Paul after that?'

His mother bridled, 'Why should he walk out? He's got no quarrel with the job. He does it well, Tremain knows that.' She reached for her empty teacup. 'He nearly got himself killed doing it today.'

Her face crumpled and Jenny jumped up. 'Let me pour you some tea.'

'Thank you, my dear.' The cup clattered in the saucer as Sarah Perrie held it. As Jenny took it from her she said shakily, 'That seems to be all I've done today, drink tea and drop dishes.'

'All's well that ends well,' said Jenny.

'Thank God it did,' said Rolf's mother, and Lorraine came in and echoed that after her.

'But he's going to be all right,' said Lorraine. 'He really is.' She was half laughing, half crying, and Jenny, pondering whether to pour tea for Lorraine too, decided it might be better to get her home.

Jenny was beginning to feel the strain herself. She would not be sorry to put her head on her own pillow and call this a day. She said, 'We ought to be getting back.'

'Yes, of course,' Lorraine was amenable now. She flung her arms around Mrs. Perrie, and was hugged in return, and when Mr. Perrie came in she said, 'We're off now,' giving him a dewy-eyed smile.

He asked, 'Did you walk here? I can't see your car.'

'Yes,' said Jenny.

Mrs. Perrie nodded meaningly at her husband. So Lorraine had had to sneak out like a thief in the night to see Rolf.

'I'll run you back,' said Mr. Perrie.

They got into his car and soon he had them at the gates of Moidores. There he stopped the car and asked Lorraine, 'Would you like to get out here?'

She said quickly, 'Yes, please.'

'Right then,' he said. 'Out with you.' They got out and thanked him, and he turned the car and drove home again, reflecting that she was a pretty lass and a nice lass, but she still didn't seem to have a spark of spirit.

Once in the house, having slipped in by a side door, Lorraine announced, 'I'm going up to my room, my head's starting to ache. I'll see you in the morning.'

She looked all in. Jenny could see she would need time before she could face any sort of questions, even from Ebby or Eb. And if Paul should loom up the pretence of having gone down to Tremain wouldn't last a minute.

'Sleep well,' said Jenny, nearing exhaustion herself.

She looked in on Timothy, who had kicked off the bedclothes but appeared none the worse for it, and tucked him in again. Then she went down into the kitchen. No one seemed to suspect them there. The only thing puzzling Ebby was why they were back so soon, and Jenny explained that Lorraine had a headache so she had come back for a reasonably early night.

Ebby sympathized and went up with headache pills and a drink, so Lorraine could still find herself either fibbing or confessing.

The whole thing had been rather idiotic and Jenny was tired. Bed for me too, she thought. She said goodnight to Eb, then remembered a magazine left in the drawing room and went to collect it.

There she parted the curtains a little to look at the sea. There wasn't much light from the room, the clouds were still low, but the sound of the sea reached her like a singing in her own blood. She opened the window and listened to it and she was at the window when Paul came into the room.

'Do you need air?' he asked.

'No. I was listening to the sea.' She closed the window and pulled the curtains back into place.

'How was the patient?'

She shrugged. 'As comfortable as you can be with a smashed foot.' She hadn't seen Rolf herself, but Paul obviously knew where they had been and splitting hairs wouldn't help.

'I gather she's reassured he's not on the danger list?'

'Yes,' said Jenny.

Paul sat down, in the leather armchair. 'I don't want that affair starting up again.'

'*You* don't?'

'It wouldn't be in Lorraine's interests.'

'Her happiness or her social position?'

'Her happiness, of course.'

'And you'd know about that better than she would?'

'Yes.' The arrogance of that shocked her deeply. She came from the window and stood looking at him. 'Did you threaten to sack Rolf Perrie?'

'Let's say I told them I wasn't prepared to subsidize them. Either through Perrie's career or through Lorraine's allowance.'

'Lorraine's allowance?'

'She has nothing of her own.'

'She doesn't own the shop? She doesn't own anything?'

'That's right.'

'And you don't think Rolf Perrie is good enough for her?'

'She didn't think so herself until today. Now there's a risk that she'll sentimentalize the situation out of control.'

Jenny protested, 'She was very distressed today – she's very fond of Rolf. She says if you'd left them alone she'd have realized before that she loved him.' Paul stayed impassive. 'But she believes you'd victimize him and his family if she went against your wishes.'

'Does she?'

'Would you?'

'That remains to be seen.' He looked grim enough. 'Don't encourage her.'

'What do you mean "encourage her"?'

She knew the signs of irascibility. He thought she was being deliberately dull-witted, and if he lost his temper she couldn't guarantee hers.

He said very slowly, 'Don't listen to her, don't let her make a confidante of you.'

'And what am I supposed to do if she wants to talk about Rolf? Snap her head off?'

'I'm sure you can deal with the situation.'

She remembered yesterday and thought – I'm less equipped for dealing with emotional situations than you imagine. Jack Bastaple will tell you I can run amok. Although why he should think anyone needs to protect you I can't imagine.

'And don't let yourself get talked into playing the go-between,' said Paul wearily. 'You've acted like a couple of silly schoolgirls today.'

How dared he? What did he think she had been doing – getting a vicarious kick out of Lorraine's thwarted romance? Lorraine had said, 'Paul laid down the law for Caterine.' And for Rolf and Lorraine. Now for Jenny.

She said, 'Those are my orders?'

'Call them what you like.'

'No,' she blazed, 'oh no! You may be the last word here, but not for me. You don't rule me, I'm not Lorraine and I am not Caterine!'

As she said it she froze. She saw the impatience leave him and he was calm and deadly cold. He said, 'Indeed you are not Caterine,' and she knew she had said the one thing that was unforgivable.

CHAPTER SIX

NEXT morning Jenny went alone to Lorraine's room as soon as she woke, before Timmy woke. It was daylight, but only just. She leaned over the silent figure and hissed, 'Lorraine!' and Lorraine yawned into the pillow and asked:

'What is it?'

'Paul knows where we were last night.'

Lorraine made a groaning noise that ended up, 'Wouldn't you know? How did he find out?'

'Worked it out, I should think,' said Jenny. 'He gave me a lecture that made me feel about two inches high and said we'd been behaving like silly schoolgirls.'

If he had phrased it differently Jenny might have agreed. It had been silly, pretending to go down to the harbour while they scurried over the heath to the Perrie's farm.

Lorraine said nothing and Jenny said, 'You are listening? You haven't gone to sleep again?'

'I'm listening.'

'Well, this is your business, of course, but can I tell you what I'd do if I were you?'

'Yes?'

'I think Paul expects you to make a great fuss, so I should play it as cool as I could. You and Rolf are friends, no one's trying to stop that, so take it from there until you're a hundred per cent sure.'

Lorraine laughed ruefully, 'That was what Rolf said.' Lorraine was impulsive and yesterday she had been prepared to promise anything. 'They were almost his words – don't make a drama out of it.'

That didn't sound like a man in love, although perhaps it did sound like a man who was not going to be hurt again.

'Could you come down to the shop this afternoon?' Lorraine asked.

'I don't know. You're going to see Rolf?'

'It's all above board, I won't pretend I'm going riding.'

Jenny said, 'I'll try,' and as she turned to go Lorraine called after her:

'Jenny, I'm ninety-nine per cent sure.'

Jenny laughed, 'That's a pretty good start!' She padded barefoot back along the carpeted corridor to the nursery and her own room. Lorraine could smile this morning, she and Rolf were starting again. This time the friendship might grow, or it might not, but they did have a second chance to make up their minds and Jenny wished them well.

She didn't feel much like smiling herself. She felt wretched and she knew why — that scene with Paul. She would have given months of her life not to have been in the drawing room last night when he'd passed the open door. She had woken this morning with a knot of misery where her heart ought to be, and for the first time since she came to Moidores she had woken feeling lonely.

Timmy was sitting up now, more asleep than awake, and she went over and hugged him. There was plenty of time and the child was warm in her arms and she needed warmth. He liked being hugged, when he was sleepy and not on his male dignity, so he snuggled against her now and fell asleep again.

She stayed with an arm around him until it really was time he was up, then she said, 'Hey, lazybones, you'll be missing the bus!'

She pulled the counterpane off him and he glared up at her, awake now, doing one of their morning routines. 'Auntie Jen, I hate you!'

'I hate you.' She gave back a ferocious scowl, and they both dissolved into giggles, and it was a way of saying, 'I love you.'

As Timmy rolled out of bed Jenny knew she wasn't lonely, she had a child for whom she would have died. But she went down to breakfast still wishing she hadn't gone to collect that magazine from the drawing room last night.

Paul was at the breakfast table. He looked up from his newspaper and said 'Good morning,' then went back to his reading, and Jenny sat down with Timmy and tipped cornflakes into his bowl and poured milk and sprinkled sugar.

There was no mention of last night. Paul was immersed in a slab of small print, no more aware of Jenny than if he had been alone. She didn't exist for him. Caterine would have talked, no one ever ignored Caterine. She would have asked, 'What's in the papers, darling? Not that dreary old political leader you're reading, what are the headlines?'

Whether she cared or not what was happening in the world she wouldn't have sat quietly by Timmy, she would have had Paul reading the newspaper to her.

... 'Indeed you are not Caterine,' he had said, and then 'Good night', so curtly that Jenny had almost run from the room, horrified at her own clumsiness. Why hadn't she stopped to think before she'd said, 'You don't rule me ... I am not Caterine.' She had been tired and indignant, and there were excuses for losing her temper. But not for losing her head so that she had not considered how her words would wound. Because Paul had overruled Caterine she had driven that car to her death. He had lost her for ever.

In her own room Jenny had looked at her reflection in the little swinging mirror on top of the chest of drawers. She was not Caterine, in any way at all. She could hear Caterine laughing at the thought, head thrown back, as she must have laughed at Lorraine and her 'ploughboy'. 'Caterine will always be here,' Lorraine had said. 'She loved this house ...'

But now Jenny sat with Timmy, facing Paul over the breakfast table. When Paul got up he ruffled Timmy's hair and gave Jenny a brief nod. Usually he said, 'See you later,' to Jenny, that meant some time during the morning in the office. This morning he said nothing to her.

Timmy had been chattering about the mine accident all through breakfast, it was going to be the big thing on the school bus this morning. Several of his schoolmates had fathers who worked in the mine and who had helped in the rescue operations.

The bus stopped to collect the children at the top of the turning for the harbour. When school had started again after the holiday Jenny had walked along with Timmy each morning, but most of the children came up the hill-side unaccompanied and Timmy had said after a few days, 'I can go on my own, you know.' Now he did, unless Lorraine was going down to Tremain at the same time.

He was passing the spot of the accident, but habit and a child's resilience seemed to have taken the terror from it. The mended fencing had matured now, the grass and bushes no longer showed signs of a car out of control.

Timmy set off for school, and Lorraine – who decided she didn't want any breakfast – set off for the shop, and Jenny went into the office.

Both Mr. Morrison and Paul were there. It wasn't quite nine o'clock and the morning mail had just arrived. They were going through it as Jenny sat down at the smallest desk, which had been brought in for her when she went on the payroll, and waited.

As soon as all the mail was opened and Paul had glanced through it he said, 'Right then, I'll see you later.'

'Where's he gone?' Jenny asked Mr. Morrison.

'To the mine.'

There was plenty to be done here. Mr. Morrison dic-tated letters, and produced papers for filing, and then while Jenny went to collect his mid-morning coffee and arrowroot biscuits got together his notes for an interview with the Inland Revenue this afternoon, and she typed those out for him too.

At lunchtime she said, 'Are you both out this after-noon?'

'Yes.'

'If I'm through here can I go and help in the shop?'

'Of course.' He had been nodding happily over his neatly typed pages; now he looked up to say, 'Miss Tre-main will be sick-visiting, I presume?'

Both he and Paul seemed to have Lorraine's plan of campaign summed up. Jenny said nothing, she wasn't giving out information, and Mr. Morrison went on, 'I should advise you not to get yourself involved in that affair.'

'I've been advised,' said Jenny. 'I've been ordered.'

Mr. Morrison made a silent 'Oh!' and Jenny demanded, 'Why should Paul dictate who Lorraine marries? He pleased himself, didn't he? Caterine hadn't a bean, but they were happy.'

In the months of working for Joe Morrison Jenny had learned to interpret the merest change of expression. To most he seemed to have no change of expression, but to Jenny now he looked sceptical.

She said quietly, 'You didn't like my sister, did you?'

'What gives you that idea?'

Caterine had not liked him, and dislike is usually mutual. Jenny said, 'She thought you didn't,' and he said briskly:

'Mrs. Tremain was a charming young lady, everybody liked her,' and went back to the notes she had typed for him.

He would hardly be likely to admit it now, and there was no point saying, 'Everyone did like Caterine. And she seemed to like everyone here but you. Why didn't she like you?'

Because Mr. Morrison had always been kind to Jenny and Jenny liked him. Caterine did not trust him, but Jenny did. Jenny would have said he had complete integrity.

He put his notes in his briefcase and said good-bye.

Grace was in the shop with Lorraine and they were starting to stocktake. During the winter months the place would be redecorated, and most of the time a notice would advise anyone seeing anything that interested them to apply to Number Three, The Close — Grace's house. Only the most hardy of tourists came down into Tremain in the winter months.

Lorraine beamed as Jenny walked in. 'Good, you got away.'

'Yes.' She dumped her handbag and took off her coat, carrying it into the little back office to hang behind the door. 'Paul's over at the mine. I asked Mr. Morrison and he said he presumed you were sick-visiting.' She mimicked Joe Morrison's caustic comment, and Lorraine and Grace smiled.

'That's right,' said Lorraine gaily. 'I'm taking grapes and goodies.' She was looking very pretty, there was a glow on her, and she couldn't get away quick enough. She went off, almost running along the quayside, her coat flying wide, and Jenny said:

'She's used up more energy yesterday and today than in all the weeks since I came here. She doesn't seem to have stopped rushing since that phone call about the accident.'

'I noticed,' said Grace. 'We've brought the stocktaking forward three weeks, although I wouldn't say it won't have to be done again.' She picked up the clipboard on which Lorraine had been making her list and drew a heart-with-arrow in the top right-hand corner.

'Love suits her,' said Jenny.

'Love?' Grace made the word a question.

'What else?'

'If it's the same as last time,' said Grace, 'they like each other, but not quite enough.'

'You knew about the last time?'

'Not till the balloon went up.' Grace had been counting rings, slotted into velvet trays, six trays to a drawer. Jenny let her get through the tray she was on now, and put down the numbers in the columns, then she asked:

'Was there much fuss?'

Grace shook her head. 'Surprisingly little. I suppose I know Lorraine as well as anybody, I've worked in here on and off almost as long as she's been running the shop. I knew she went out with Rolf Perrie sometimes, but it seems they'd known each other since they were kids, and no one made anything of that. Not until Caterine started teasing her about him.'

Grace sounded accusing and Jenny said, 'Caterine always teased. She wouldn't mean to hurt Lorraine or cause trouble.'

Grace snorted, 'Well, she managed to do both.' She took out another tray of rings and said, 'After that we heard no more about Rolf Perrie from Lorraine. He stopped coming down to the harbour and Lorraine started dating in the higher income bracket, the Tremain circuit, Caterine's friends.'

'Weren't you Caterine's friends?'

'Of course,' said Grace. 'But in the lower income bracket.' She took out a ring that looked like a great gold nugget, except that it was rather brighter than gold. 'What happened to all Caterine's jewellery? She had a ring like this, but the real thing. She had some fantastic stuff.'

Bracelets and pearls, Jenny had seen them in the painting. She knew about Caterine's jewellery. Caterine usually brought some of it along with her when she came on holiday.

'Paul always bought her jewellery,' Jenny said. 'Birthdays and Christmases and anniversaries. Always. I suppose jewellery is an investment that never loses its value, but sometimes I should think she'd have liked a change, a surprise.'

Grace looked at her quickly. 'You're joking! Caterine never wanted anything except a bigger bracelet.' Then, as though that had to be softened a little, 'And why not? So would I if I had the chance. You know what Ben bought me for my last birthday?'

'What?'

'A cooker, with a box of chocolates on the top shelf. And I turned on the oven without spotting the chocolates. We got them out before the wrappings set on fire, but not before they'd all melted into each other. So then we put them in the fridge, and they made a very unusual pudding.'

Jenny laughed, her thoughts grave. Everybody was Caterine's friend. But not Mr. Morrison, and neither, without reservations, was Grace Norwood. Grace would not have spoken like that immediately after the accident, but the charisma of death was fading.

Of course Caterine would have been envied. She was

outstandingly beautiful, and rich. It was a wonder she had any friends at all, outside the ones with whom she was on close and intimate terms. The rest would just envy her, and not know how warm and generous she was, how loving.

Jenny had adored Caterine all her life. It saddened her hearing anyone blaming Caterine for anything, but defending a memory would only remind her how much she herself had lost.

Grace had just told the joke about the chocolates to change the subject, and Grace was not the only one who could be tactless and then wish that she hadn't.

So Jenny smiled and asked, 'How do you stocktake?' and listened carefully while Grace explained and gave her Lorraine's list to re-check.

They had the place almost to themselves for the next hour or two. They talked about the excitement at the mine yesterday. Grace knew what Jenny didn't know, that Paul had been the one to climb through the clearing in the rubble and go to find Rolf Perrie.

Most of the men working at the mine lived in Tremain. Yesterday everyone had waited: not only the miners' families, but artists, tradesmen, fishermen. And when it was all over every detail had been avidly discussed.

Grace knew much more than Jenny. That a single bolt in the coupling of a truck had given way causing the truck to crash down, uncontrolled, leaving the track and smashing into the timber supports. Just one bolt.

That while the men worked, clearing a way, there had been other falls, and when there was a passage through somehow there had been no question that Paul Tremain was going into the darkness to find Rolf Perrie.

He had gone through before it was safe. No one had been certain what state Rolf was in. He had spoken on the phone hours earlier and been told to get back, well away from the fall. He had understood and said he would, but he had sounded groggy and finished, 'Make it as soon as you can.'

As soon as there was room to get through Paul Tremain had gone. The assistant manager had protested, 'What do we do if it comes down again and you're both in there?' and Paul had grinned and said, 'Carry on digging, for God's sake.'

That, said Grace, had struck them all as very funny. They were still laughing at that when Paul came back practically carrying Rolf, and the miners hadn't finished grinning over it yet.

'Do you think it's funny?' Grace asked.

'No,' said Jenny. She went on, without quite knowing why, 'Paul wasn't joking when I saw him last night. He was very short-tempered.'

'He'd had a tiring day,' said Grace, and with that Jenny had to agree.

Grace was totting up things in the window when Jack Bastaple walked by. She tapped the window and called to Jenny, 'Here's Jack!' and Jenny retreated further into the shop, ending up by the door to the office with a hand on the knob.

But Jack didn't even glance towards the shop and Grace queried in surprise, 'What's got into him?'

'He thinks I might be in here.' Jenny moved forward again. 'We had a disagreement on Saturday about one of his pictures.'

Grace grinned with cheerful malice, 'Well, if you didn't like it he'll sulk until you say you've changed your mind and you're sorry.'

But an apology wouldn't put the canvas back together, and Jenny had as little to say to Jack as he had to say to her. It would suit Jenny if they both kept their distance.

Grace may have thought she was being diplomatic, or it could just have been coincidence an hour or so later. There were customers in, and Grace was showing them jewellery, but she suddenly said in an aside to Jenny, 'Ask Ben to turn the casserole on, there's a dear. He's in the studio.'

'Shall I turn it on?' Jenny suggested.

'No,' said Grace, 'he understands the oven.'

If it was a new cooker it should do what the dials said, but Grace was giving an animated sales talk about pendants, swinging one with a multi-coloured stone the better to catch the light; so Jenny went to the studio, although she had a sinking feeling that was where Jack Bastaple had been going.

This afternoon it was very much the clubhouse atmosphere. There were paintings around, unfinished models and sculptures on the benches, but most of the artists were sitting down drinking coffee. There was no hurry any more, the fast-selling season was over.

Jenny knew them all, they greeted her as she went in, and one girl waved a mug at her. 'Cup of coffee, Jen?'

'No, thanks,' said Jenny. She called, 'Ben, message from Grace.'

Ben Norwood was at the far end from the door, in his usual spot, sitting on the edge of a working bench, with a block of basalt beside him. Jack was there too, painting, and Jenny needed to pass Jack to reach Ben.

She hesitated briefly, but it would have been ridiculous to yell, and she began to walk the length of the barny old room.

What was Jack painting? If it was Caterine again it would lose its impact if his colleagues watched him paint it. Jenny wouldn't look unless she had to, she would just walk down to Ben and ask him to go home and turn on the oven.

But as she passed Jack he growled, 'You're not curious?'

So she stopped. It was not Caterine. It was an abstract of slashing colours. She could imagine it as a therapy for anger. He gave her no chance to speak, and what could she have said if he had? But he looked at her much as he had done on Saturday and walked past her, out of the studio, the steel tips on his heels clattering on the iron staircase outside.

The girl who had offered her coffee, the mother of Leah one of Timmy's friends, said, 'So it was you.'

'What was?'

'Our Jack's foul mood. What have you done to him?'

Jenny said again, 'I didn't like a picture he'd painted. We had a row.' And they all smiled; Jack Bastaple's touchiness about his work was well-known.

'Which was it?' someone else asked, and Jenny said:

'A sea picture,' and reached Ben Norwood. 'Please, Grace said would you turn on the casserole?'

'This very minute,' said Ben Norwood cheerfully. He was a man of medium height, grey-haired, thick-set, with bright kind eyes in a round face. He went out with Jenny, and at the bottom of the steps he asked, 'Was that why Grace sent you in, to patch up the quarrel?'

'I suspect it was,' said Jenny. 'But it wasn't so much a quarrel as a long farewell.'

Ben laughed and clapped her on the shoulder and said, 'Tell Grace that or she'll be getting you both round to supper.'

'If she did it would probably choke Jack.'

'Would you care?'

'Of course,' said Jenny. 'Well, perhaps not much,' and she went back into the shop while Ben was still laughing.

Grace was finishing her sale. When the customers had gone she turned an inquiring look on Jenny. Jenny said, 'Ben's switching on the oven right now,' and without any pretence of gaiety, 'Jack was there. He walked out of the studio as I walked in.'

And then she told Grace about the painting of Caterine as the chained sea witch. 'He wouldn't sell it to me, he'd painted it for his exhibition; he was determined it was getting the biggest audience going, and it was terrifying. I think it would have given Timmy nightmares again if he'd ever seen it.'

'Jack's a young fool,' said Grace, her tolerance strained. 'What's his idea?'

'He said Paul kept Caterine prisoner. Jack wanted to remind everybody that she didn't escape.' She swallowed and it hurt. 'She died, but she didn't escape.'

'Prisoner my eye!' Grace exploded. 'Caterine Tremain had a marvellous life!'

'I know, but Jack thinks that Paul shouldn't have stopped her acting. She did have tremendous talent, I suppose she should have used it.'

'Then she shouldn't have married a possessive man,'

118

said Grace, 'and I think she was flattered that he wanted to keep her with him. She'd talk about the offers she'd had, but I'm sure she enjoyed saying, "Paul would never let me".'

That had been Jenny's impression over all the years of Caterine's marriage. Until just before the accident she was certain that Caterine had never really tried to make Paul change his mind. Jenny said huskily, 'It looked like someone looking through bars.'

'Did it?' Grace pulled a wry face. 'I've got to see this.'

'You haven't heard it all.' What Jenny had to say now would probably sound like murder to an artist. 'I ripped it up.'

Someone screeched suddenly outside the shop, the children were home from school, and Jenny and Grace both jumped. Then Grace gulped, 'You *did*?'

'With the bread knife.'

Grace groped for the chair behind her and backed into it. 'That must have been a lulu of a scene!'

'I shouldn't like it to happen again,' admitted Jenny bleakly. 'Not that it will, he's not likely to let me get near to it a second time, but he said he'd paint it again.'

'Silly lad!' Grace sighed. 'He's always had this chip on his shoulder about Paul Tremain. He still hankers for the old days when this was a fishing village and nothing else. To hear him talk you'd think it was heaven on earth before Paul Tremain turned it into big business.'

Perhaps it was, thought Jenny. When Jack Bastaple was a boy and it was peaceful all year round, except for the sea and the seabirds. She said quietly, 'Perhaps Paul has spoiled Tremain,' but Grace, innately practical, was not having that.

'How has he spoiled it?' she demanded. 'The harbour's the same, the houses are the same. The only difference is that the mine's being worked again, and in the summer the tourists come. And while Jack's being snide about the tourists he's quick enough to take their money.' She warmed to her argument, with a flourishing gesture for the layout of the shop. 'There wouldn't be much point in a place like this, would there, unless somebody was going to look and buy?'

There were three of Jack's pictures displayed for sale, and several more stacked in the office. Jenny knew them all, but she went across now and looked again at the one of the old mine entrance.

The old mine was always a popular subject, and Jack's painting brought out the gold of gorse and the purple of heather, made the grass greener and emphasized the texture of the crumbling stonework. She asked Grace, who was a professional and ought to know, 'He is good, isn't he?'

'Much better than average,' said Grace. She leaned back in her chair, casting a critical eye at the picture Jenny was viewing. 'But he's no Van Gogh, so I shouldn't worry about having deprived the world of a masterpiece. By the way, can I tell Ben?'

She would anyway, but if Jenny asked it would go no further than that. Jenny said, 'Yes, but please don't tell anyone else. If everyone knows Jack will have to paint Caterine again, out of bravado. But if no one says anything he might decide not to bother.'

'Don't rely on it.' Grace had known Jack a long time. 'This could seem the best chance he's ever had for knocking Tremain.'

It would be unpleasant for Paul, Jenny agreed, but it was Timothy she was worried about. 'It would be so bad for Timmy.'

'Yes, I see that.' Grace got up and shoved the little gilt-cane chair back against the counter irritably, as though she was shaking Jack. 'The man's a menace!' She grinned, her white uneven teeth flashing against the tan of her skin. 'We could always pretend it was a painting of you, not Caterine.'

'Me?' Jenny smiled too. 'Oh no, it wasn't me. It was very much Caterine, and it was good of her, except that Caterine was nobody's prisoner.'

'If it was good of her it was like you,' said Grace. She gave Jenny the same impersonal appraisal she had just given the painting of the old mine. 'One tends to forget how much you do look like her. You don't talk like her, nor act like her, but feature for feature you certainly look like her.'

'*No,*' said Jenny.

'Especially now your hair's longer.' It hadn't been cut since Jenny came here. It touched her shoulders now, dark and softly waving.

From deep inside Jenny something said with longing, 'I wish I was like Caterine,' and Grace's lips parted to say:

'You—' then she bit her lip and smiled, 'What for? All that jewellery?'

'I wouldn't bother about the stones,' said Jenny gaily. 'I'm a junk jewellery girl.' She picked up one of the pendants left on the counter from the selection Grace had been showing the last customers and admired it. 'This is my idea of a super piece.'

What would she want that had been Caterine's? She wouldn't let herself think. She said, 'School's out.'

'You want to get back?' Grace suggested. 'It's all right if you do.'

'I think I will.' Jenny got her coat from the office, and Ben came in through the side door from the courtyard and asked,

'How many for supper?'

'Just us,' said Grace. She looked across at Jenny and Jenny said:

'Do explain to Ben that I don't make a habit of it.'

She meant, destroying paintings, and Grace said, 'Oh, I will, I will.'

'A habit of what?' asked Ben, intrigued. He came over to his wife, a comfortable not particularly ambitious man, doing work he enjoyed among people he liked, sharing everything with Grace.

Tremain suits them, thought Jenny, or is it that they suit each other?

She said good-bye and walked out on to the quayside, looking across the water and waving at Dan Blaskie rowing in from the *Mylor*. Beyond the *Mylor* loomed the Witch's Rock. Jenny hadn't been out to the Rock since she came to Tremain this time, but she believed she remembered everything about it: the tiny cove, secure and hidden from wind and wave, the honeycomb of caves.

Reaching it required masterly seamanship, because of tide-race and submerged rocks most ships kept clear, but she had been taken there for a picnic once when she and Lorraine were schoolgirls, and the caves had been a magic land to Jenny.

She wondered now whether the years between had broken the spell. One day she might find out. No one had changed the Witch's Rock as Paul Tremain had changed the world of Jack Bastaple's boyhood. In Jack's eyes that would always be a lost Shangri-La.

As she passed the side street where Jack lived Jenny was filled with exasperated pity for him. Because if he was in the cottage painting that portrait again he was hurting himself more than he could ever hurt Paul.

'I remember the eyes,' Jack had said, but the eyes he had painted had been agonized. From time to time Caterine had yearned a little for the career she might have had. When she'd talked about it of course she had portrayed her emotions vividly: she was a born actress. But there had been no agony. Jack had exaggerated, like painting grass greener than it grew and the shadowy entrance to the old mine black as pitch.

Jenny knew what Caterine's reaction would have been to that painting. She would have stared at it, and at the man who had painted it, and then she would have laughed. . . .

Lorraine came home looking happy. Not deliriously, but bathed in a quiet content. She had been at the Perries all afternoon, had helped Rolf's mother get the tea, and she had fetched and carried trays for the invalid.

Paul had been there in the morning, and so had the doctor, and Rolf was fine.

She told them all this in the kitchen, and meeting Ebby's worried frown she teased, 'Don't fuss, Ebby, we're not going to elope. We wouldn't get far unless I wheeled him in a wheelbarrow.'

'What's "elope"?' Timmy tugged Jenny's sleeve and Ebby said dourly:

'A passel of trouble.'

'Run away,' said Lorraine, smiling, and Jenny felt Timmy's fingers tighten around the stuff of her sleeve.

That night when he was in bed he said, 'Auntie Jen, you wouldn't ever elope, would you?' and she had to explain that elope did not mean disappearance, desertion; it meant getting married.

'Oh, is that all?' He seemed reassured, and as she turned to leave the room and go downstairs again he said, 'And if you did get married you'd marry someone from here, wouldn't you?'

'Would I?'

'Oh yes.' She hid a smile when he followed that with, 'You don't want to get married yet, but you'll find somebody before you're old, and if you don't I'll look after you.'

Downstairs she said to Lorraine, 'Do you see any grey hairs? Timmy's planning my old age, but not to worry because if I can't get anyone to marry me he's going to look after me.'

Within a fortnight Rolf Perrie was hobbling around the farmhouse with the aid of a stick. Branch Three of the tin mine, which he had been inspecting because it was almost worked out, had been sealed and another seam opened up. The excitement was over, routine was re-established at the mine, and the patient was recovering at a gratifying rate.

Lorraine and Rolf had not eloped, and Jenny saw no sign that they were likely to when Rolf was mobile again, although Lorraine went over to the Perries' farm most evenings.

She went openly now. Paul knew she was a constant visitor, everyone knew, but he didn't seem to object. He even gave her a folder of papers once to deliver to Rolf, as though there was no longer any risk or danger in the relationship. Jenny, who saw them together from time to time, would have described it all as cosy as an old slipper.

Rolf had plenty of callers, he was well liked, but when Lorraine was the only visitor they did crosswords and played chess and listened to records. So Lorraine told

Jenny, and when Jenny went along there was the chessboard, and Jenny could believe it.

Mrs. Perrie was nicer these days, much friendlier, and an evening at the Perries' was pleasant, but there was nothing electric in the air. Rolf's welcome for Lorraine was hardly a lover's. A good friend's, yes, someone very glad to see her; and Lorraine enjoyed fussing around Rolf, helping to look after him.

He humoured her, and their affection for each other seemed genuine enough, but it was not a passion. Jenny couldn't imagine them defying Paul, and risking Rolf's job or anything else to be together. They seemed a pair who might have drifted into marriage and been happy enough, so long as no difficulties were put in their way.

So Paul need not have read the riot act the night of the accident, because Lorraine was not going to need a go-between nor a confidante. And if Paul hadn't bullied her Jenny would not have said what she did – and the times she had regretted that, because ever since that night Paul had been unapproachable.

She worked with him in the office, ate meals with him, sometimes – not often – sat in the evenings, reading, watching television, and beneath the surface there was no point of contact at all.

No one else realized that, not even Mr. Morrison. Paul talked to Jenny, he was never verbose with anyone, but he did address remarks to her. He spoke kindly, sharply, sometimes with humour, and Jenny answered, followed instructions, joined discussions, and all the time there was this great invisible wall.

She could do nothing about it. She was seized with a strangling shyness at the thought of wording an apology, so ill at ease in his company that she avoided him as much as she could.

She took care not to make it conspicuous. Office hours of course she was around, but when Paul worked late at nights now she didn't go into the office. If he'd asked her to work she would have done, but he never did.

She spent some of her evenings with Eb and Ebby, and some with Lorraine, or with Grace and her neighbours.

Down in Tremain Jack was still acting as though she was a plague-carrier, to the amusement of his colleagues. 'What is this picture all the fuss is about?' one rather spiteful soul had inquired, and been thunderously asked what the hell he was talking about.

'Whether Jack is painting it again I wouldn't know,' Grace said to Jenny. 'If he is he's painting it at home, not in the studio.'

Grace and Ben were still the only ones who knew that the painting had been of Caterine. Lorraine had no idea, and she still thought the breach between Jenny and Jack was a pity. As Jack walked past them on the quayside one Friday afternoon, staring rigidly ahead, Lorraine said with smothered laughter, 'You certainly turned him off, and you could have done with some company this weekend.'

Next day Lorraine was taking Timmy to a birthday party and they were staying overnight. 'It looks as if I'll have to manage without Jack,' said Jenny. 'Hi, Dan!'

Dan Blaskie was making for the jetty, carrying a cardboard box full of provisions. He was brown and tough as old leather, and when he reached the two girls he grinned, jaws clamped on a short dirty-looking clay pipe. He always had a smile for Lorraine and a joke for Jenny. Today he put down the cardboard box, took his pipe out of his mouth, and inquired, 'Do ee fancy a trip round the bay, m'dear?'

'You're on,' said Jenny. 'Where are we going?' She looked at the *Mylor* that was Dan's pride and joy, and he said smugly:

'She's a good ole sea-boat, is that. You could go round the Cape in ur.'

'When?' sàid Jenny. She laughed and Dan said:

'Have to see the skipper, but he don't belong to have passengers messin' around. He goes to get away from 'em.'

'Get away from what?' Jenny joked. 'Not the Tremain estates, surely. I wonder he can bear to leave them.'

'Do ee, m'dear?' The sailor's keen eyes were hooded. 'And he wonders how he can stomach comin' back to 'em.' He chuckled as he spoke. Lorraine was smiling a sweet vague smile, paying only slight attention, but Jenny looked hard at him, and he picked up his box again and said, 'Young Perrie still comin' on all right, then?'

Another few days and Rolf would be taking over his desk duties again at the mine. He had been doing some work from home, but he was a restless invalid, intolerant of his disability.

Last night Jenny had been at the Perries', sitting in the parlour with Rolf and Lorraine, when the phone rang in the hall and Mr. Perrie had shouted, 'Rolf!'

Rolf had reached for his stick, and Lorraine, jumping up and holding out a hand, had said, 'Come on, lean on me.'

'I can manage.'

She watched him with a crooked smile, then she said quietly, 'Scared I'll let you down?'

Rolf had smiled too, and walked with the aid of his stick slowly and carefully out of the room to answer the phone. . . .

In the office this morning Jenny had said to Mr. Morrison, 'I can't think why anyone worried about that affair setting light. Rolf's more like Lorraine's brother than her brother is.' Paul had always seemed more like his sister's guardian to Jenny.

Mr. Morrison did his slight shrug, and Jenny went on, 'Paul knows that, of course. Does he have his spies?'

That shocked Mr. Morrison, although how else would Paul know? and Jenny couldn't resist teasing, 'Because if he does he'll hear that I'm carrying the love-letters this weekend.' Then she relented, 'It's all right, I'm only taking a book. Lorraine doesn't think Rolf can exist till Monday night without another thriller.'

Jenny thought he could. He had said he had books he hadn't finished reading, but this was a new one by a favourite author, and Lorraine had said, 'Jenny, would you bring it on Saturday?'

'Of course,' Jenny had said. But she was sure that Rolf would have survived the weekend without the book, and she was equally sure he would survive the weekend without Lorraine. . . .

Jenny rarely worked Saturday mornings, although Paul and Mr. Morrison did. After breakfast Lorraine and Timmy drove away for the birthday party, and Jenny enjoyed her walk over the heathland to the Perries' farm. She was having lunch and spending the rest of the weekend with Grace and Ben, and the weather was frosty and exhilarating. She walked fast, getting colour into her cheeks.

Mrs. Perrie, aproned for housework, answered the door, and Jenny would have handed in the book with a few words, but Mrs. Perrie insisted on her coming in for a cup of tea.

The cup of tea was in the kitchen with Rolf, his mother was busy with upstairs chores. He had working papers on the table and he put down the book beside them, and said, 'Thank you, but you shouldn't have bothered.'

'I promised Lorraine. She was very anxious you should have it.'

'She was, wasn't she?' He picked the book up again and frowned. He was looking at the picture on the dust jacket, but Jenny felt he was not seeing it. He asked, 'Where has she gone, Jenny?'

'She told you. She's taken Timmy to a birthday party. The Lawrences, their little girl Susan is ten.'

'Oh yes,' said Rolf mockingly, 'the Lawrences.'

When Caterine had given parties at Moidores the Lawrences were always on the guest list. Since Caterine's death there had been no entertaining, but the Lawrences had called and Jenny had met them, and they had seemed an amiable pair of upper-middle-class intellectuals. She asked, 'What's the matter with the Lawrences?'

Rolf laughed, 'There's nothing the matter with the Lawrences.' But there was something the matter with him, that was putting an edge on his voice and a bleakness in his eyes. 'They're rolling in money,' he said. 'She'll come to no harm there.'

Jenny said levelly, 'That doesn't make much sense.' Although she knew what he meant.

'Oh, but it does,' he said.

'Lorraine would rather be here with you than taking Timmy to a party.'

Neither was drinking the cups of tea that Mrs. Perrie had poured for them. Jenny held hers untasted, and Rolf's had been untouched since his mother set it down. He said cynically, 'She might at that, she's enjoyed playing Florence Nightingale,' and when Jenny tried to protest,

'You make it sound as though it's been a game to her,' he demanded:

'Well, hasn't it?'

She challenged him, 'Is it a game for you? How much do you really care for Lorraine?'

For an unguarded moment he looked lost and hopeless. He cared deeply, and it was plainer than words. Then he said, 'Too much to persuade her to give up the life she has for the life I could give her. She'd have to be tough, wouldn't she, to go with me to the kind of places I could find a job?'

She would have to be a hundred per cent sure, ninety-nine per cent wasn't enough. Jenny said, 'Did Paul threaten to sack you?' and Rolf managed a creditable grin.

'He didn't give us his blessing.'

'Would you risk it?'

'For myself? Sure I would.'

'Does Lorraine know that?'

'I told her once, and nothing's changed. It's up to Lorraine.'

She asked, 'Can I tell her that?' and he said quietly:

'Why bother? She's always known it.'

CHAPTER SEVEN

JENNY walked back to Tremain slowly, hands deep in her coat pockets, thinking, remembering Rolf's words just now and Lorraine's expression when she heard that Rolf was trapped in the mine.

There had been no pretence then. Lorraine had been racked with fear for him. But now there was no danger, and maybe Lorraine was enjoying playing Florence Nightingale.

There didn't seem to be much that Jenny could do. Suppose she told Lorraine what Rolf had just said and added her own mite of persuasion, and they did stand up to Paul and Paul did chuck Rolf out of his job?

Emigration could be an exciting challenge for some folk. Rolf could cope with it, although he'd obviously rather stay where he was. Lorraine was physically delicate; should anyone be urging her to give up a comfortable sheltered life unless her own heart dictated it overwhelmingly?

By the time Jenny crossed the cliff-top road and started down the cobblestoned track to the harbour the only resolve Jenny had reached was to leave well alone. This was between Rolf and Lorraine; no one else should interfere. Except Paul, and the only way he should interfere was by stopping the blackmail.

Think of the devil, she thought, as she reached the quayside. There were no tourists around today although it was fine and bright, because it was November and cold. Tremain must be near enough now to what it was when Jack Bastaple was a boy. No gay umbrellas outside the Tremain Arms, and locals sitting on the benches, all men, and children playing around.

One of the men standing talking was Paul Tremain, wearing a thick black sweater and reefing jacket, oil-stained trousers and gumboots. The wind made his dark thatch of hair look like Timmy's. Jenny smiled and waved – they all knew her, they all nodded at her as she rounded the Tremain Arms and came into view.

She thought – it's surprising what a change of clothing will do. This morning at breakfast you were Tremain of Tremain. Now you're a Cornish seaman, and your empire is that boat out there.

She said, 'Hello,' here and there as she walked along by the harbour wall. It was midday and she was having lunch with Grace and Ben. But first she walked out on to the jetty to where the dinghy for the *Mylor* was moored.

Her exasperation at Lorraine – who didn't seem to know what she did want – had transferred to herself. She knew that she wanted to go sailing. Paul didn't take passengers and he would say so, but she'd be no worse off than before and she was going to ask.

The freshness of the wind blowing across the sea from the north-west brought with it a zest and a sweetness that made her a little high when she breathed deeply, and the sun glittered dazzlingly on the sea and the boats and the seagulls flying; and when Paul and Dan Blaskie came along the jetty she was in such a state of euphoria that she managed to say easily and gaily, 'Dan says you don't take passengers, what are the chances for a stowaway?'

They both smiled. It was a quip, a joke, only it wasn't. Her hair blew across her face blinding her, and she held it back and pleaded, 'I'm not joking. Please will you take me with you?' That wasn't so easy, and Paul stopped smiling and said,

'The weather forecast isn't too good.'

'Foreboding ole weather, I do call it,' Dan backed him up. But he hadn't said no.

'I wouldn't be seasick.' Of course she wouldn't, although Paul was looking at her quizzically and asking:

'How much sailing have you done?'

Hugging the coastline and back for tea, and he knew it. She said desperately, 'If I am I'll hide. I'll hide all the time if you like, I'll keep right out of your way.'

'It isn't that big a boat.' He was smiling and he hadn't said no, and she said:

'I'll find somewhere. *Please!*'

'All right,' he said. 'Ask someone to phone the house and let Ebby know where you've gone.'

'I was staying with Grace Norwood, I'll tell her, I won't be a minute.' She didn't waste a second. She sped back along the jetty, through the archway and through the bright yellow front door of Grace's cottage. In the tiny hall she shouted, 'Grace!' and Grace carolled back from the kitchen:

'In here!'

'I'm going sailing with Paul and Dan – you don't mind, do you?'

Grace almost dropped the frying pan. She put it on the stove, turned down the heat and gave all her attention to Jenny. 'How did that happen?'

'I just asked Paul and he said all right.'

Grace was speechless for all of five seconds. Then she said, 'You can't sail in those shoes.'

They were stout walking shoes with smooth rubber soles for the trek over the heathlands to the Perries' farm. 'I've got another pair in my bag,' Jenny said.

She had brought down an overnight bag yesterday afternoon. It was now in Grace's spare bedroom, containing pyjamas, sponge bag, and with a dress change hanging in the wardrobe.

As Jenny ran up the stairs Grace stood at the bottom calling up after her, 'What did you *say?*'

'Could I come, and I wouldn't be seasick and if I was I'd keep out of sight.'

She wouldn't need the frock. She was in sweater and skirt under a tweed coat. She yelled, 'Grace, can you lend me some jeans?'

Grace was taller than Jenny, but narrow-hipped, and she seemed to live in jeans and trousers. She went into the other bedroom and came out with a pair of blue dungarees. 'If you roll them up round the waist they should do. Have you got time to try them on?'

'No, they'll fit. Thanks,' Jenny shoved them into the bag. 'See you tomorrow.'

'Where are you going?' Grace followed her downstairs.

'I don't know. But they always come back on Sunday, don't they?'

Grace chortled behind her, 'A night under the stars with old Dan Blaskie!'

'Don't worry about my reputation,' Jenny laughed. 'There's always Paul for chaperon.'

'Yes,' said Grace, 'there is, isn't there?'

She walked to the archway with Jenny, and Jenny gave a little cry because they hadn't waited for her. The dinghy had left the jetty and was almost at the *Mylor*, and she felt a stinging disappointment that emptied her of joy and left her hollow and sick.

It wasn't fair! She wanted to shout that after them, like an ill-treated child.

And then the void in her filled with churning anger. She dropped her bag and ran again, and Grace scooped it up and hurried after her. At the end of the jetty Grace caught up as Jenny stooped to fiddle with the buckle of her shoe. 'What are you doing?' Grace asked.

'I'm swimming out,' said Jenny.

'You are *not*!' yelped Grace as Jenny yanked off first one shoe and then the other. 'Don't be daft – it's cold, you'll get pneumonia if you don't drown.'

'I won't drown,' said Jenny. 'He'll have to pick me up, he can hardly leave me swimming out to sea.'

'He'll just bring you back. If he's changed his mind there's nothing you can do about it.'

'I can make a nuisance of myself.' Jenny unbuttoned her coat with furious fumbling fingers. 'I feel like making a nuisance of myself!'

The dinghy reached the *Mylor* and one man got aboard. The other stayed at the oars and began to row back. Grace began to laugh, almost hysterically.

Tears rolled down her cheeks until she clung to a capstan, weak with laughter, gasping, 'Oh, I wish they'd taken a minute longer. You'd have been in the water. It would have been the funniest thing—'

Jenny began to laugh too. Another couple of minutes and she would have dived in from the end of the jetty. It was idiotic that it hadn't occurred to her that they could have decided there was no point both of them waiting. She had been so sure Paul had changed his mind and was going without her. She begged, 'Stop laughing, for heaven's sake, he'll think I'm crazy,' and Grace sobbed,

'You are crazy. Get your coat and your shoes back on, they think it's a strip-tease.'

Jenny was getting a fair amount of attention. Several of the children had followed to see why she and Grace were running. If she had taken off her skirt and started swimming out they would have loved that, and Paul would have had every good reasoning for doubting her sanity.

She got shoes and coat on quickly, but each time she looked at Grace the giggles took over, and when Paul – it would be him rowing back, not Dan – drew up alongside the jetty they were still struggling to regain their composure.

He greeted Grace and helped Jenny across into the dinghy, and Grace handed over Jenny's bag and said, 'Don't – forget this,' hiccuping as she tried to hold down laughter and sounding so odd that Paul asked:

'What's the matter?'

'Not a thing,' said Grace shrilly. 'Goodbye.' She waved briefly, and turned away with shaking shoulders, and Jenny sat facing Paul.

'What is the matter?' he asked again, pushing off from the jetty.

She looked beyond him at the *Mylor* and the Witch's Rock and admitted, 'I thought you'd changed your mind and gone without me.'

'Was that what Mrs. Norwood found amusing?'

'No. I nearly dived in and swam out.'

He didn't believe her. He said, 'If I had changed my mind I'd have stayed to tell you, and I hope you weren't considering swimming.'

'I'm a strong swimmer.'

'I thought Timothy was teaching you to swim.'

'That was to get Timmy playing in the water again.' She added quietly, 'He was afraid of the sea.'

Paul knew why. She watched a seagull perched on a bobbing red buoy, and they were almost at the *Mylor* before he spoke again.

'You're not?' he asked.

'I love the sea.'

'Let's hope you feel the same way tomorrow. And when you do go swimming remember there are tides and currents here as well as rocks. You may think you're a good swimmer, but this is not a swimming pool.'

He thought she was talking boastful nonsense, and perhaps she was. It must sound like nonsense from a girl who had never been further out to sea than the Witch's Rock, on one picnic in high summer, years ago.

She promised herself, I'll be quiet from now on, you won't know I'm aboard. But when they came alongside the *Mylor* she looked at it with dazzled eyes and whispered, 'She's beautiful.'

Paul said, 'You should have seen her when I found her.'

'Wasn't she beautiful then?'

'I thought so.'

She wanted to say, 'Where? When? Tell me how you found her.' But Dan was there and Paul was saying:

'Take her down to her cabin,' and she went meekly and silently, thanking her lucky stars that she hadn't dived into the harbour. Because if she had she knew she would have been promptly landed back on the jetty and never allowed to set foot on the mellowed teak deck of the *Mylor*.

She followed Dan through a two-door hatch on the forepeak of the boat, into a small cabin with sail lockers and stores, then down a couple of steps into another cabin containing fishing gear, scuba-suit, oxygen bottles, a trunk and a hard wooden bunk.

Dan chuckled as she looked at the bunk, wondering if she would be sleeping on bare boards. 'Weren't expectin' ee, m'dear. 'Tes a snug li'l berth when it's made right. Doan't ee worry 'bout that.'

'That's a relief,' Jenny admitted.

Dan produced a seaman's waterproof coat from one of

the lockers, satisfied himself that she had a pair of non-skid shoes and left her to it. She changed into Grace's jeans, rolling them up at the waist and the coat up at the sleeves. The effect was not glamorous, but it was warm and practical, and that was all that mattered right now.

She wanted to explore. The memory of her visit to the Witch's Rock was stirred again, because she had gone into the caves with just this feeling of awe and excitement, this tingling delight. Ever since she came back to Tremain the schooner, usually anchored at the mouth of the harbour, had been like a mirage, something wonderful and unattainable, and now she was aboard she wanted to see every nook and cranny.

Another door from this cabin led past the foot of the mainmast, which came down through the decking, into the main cabin. The engine had started up now, they were moving out of harbour, and she peered through the porthole for a while, then turned back to admire the cosy comfort of the cabin.

The walls were mahogany-panelled, and when the paraffin lamps were lit the grain of the wood would glow warm. There were two wide settees with cushions and a narrow table, and a small galley and toilet leading off.

Jenny touched nothing and she went back the way she had come. She had promised not to get underfoot and she kept out of the way of both men.

Paul came looking for her once as she stood at the rail that rose in a curve around the bow of the *Mylor*. Already the coastline was a blur astern, it was warmer out at sea than back on land and the sun still shone.

'All right?' Paul asked.

She nodded, smiling.

'Good,' he said. He didn't tell her that when she first came up on deck he had said to Dan, 'Keep an eye on her. Get her to tie herself to the rails if she looks as if she might lose her footing.'

It was calm weather yet, but there was a suggestion of a swell and he felt responsible. But Dan had announced approvingly afterwards, 'Sure-footed as a cat. Moves about a boat like one reared to it.'

Jenny was moving with the boat. It was like floating, like flying. The engine had served its purpose of getting them out of harbour. Now the sails billowed and although the wind was not strong Paul was using every possible combination of sail and technique to scoop in sufficient wind to make four knots against the tide and swell.

Jenny snuggled behind the large collar of her seaman's jacket, her eyes sparkling and her skin glowing. When Dan came forward checking the rigging she asked, 'Where are we going?'

They were following a looping course which would take them about thirty-five miles offshore, out of the shipping lanes. There they would ride at anchor overnight if the weather held fair and then loop back, stopping at the Witch's Rock.

Jenny almost clapped her hands. 'The Rock?'

'The skipper allus looks in there if it's only for an hour. Though this ain't no time o' year for sailing in to Witch's Rock.'

But he didn't seem particularly perturbed by the prospect and Jenny was delighted. As Dan stuffed his short clay pipe with tobacco she said, 'Of course we'll make it. *Mylor*'s a good ship.'

His weathered wrinkled face with its dark tan cracked in a smile. 'You're right there, m'dear. No malice in ur.' Jenny understood what he meant. The *Mylor* would obey the helm and return loving care, that she would ride the sea without harshness as if she was part of the sea.

'And the skipper's a good seaman,' said Dan. 'He respects the sea. He could take a boat through the eye of a needle.'

The short daylight hours passed as *Mylor* dipped and curtseyed on the waves, and Jenny leaned over the bows, secured by a rope, looking for fish and hoping to see a dolphin. Once she thought she had, just ahead of the bows, but it turned out to be a school of smaller fish.

With the coming of darkness came an appreciable chill and she moved aft as the light failed, and stood for a while on the afterdeck behind the partly covered wheelhouse where Paul was still at the wheel.

She saw the first stars come out, and in a short time the whole sky was ablaze. Jenny could only stare. She had never known how wonderful a clear night at sea could be on a crisp cloudless November night.

She stood enraptured, watching a shooting star, trying to make out the pattern of the planets. She found the Plough and the North Star. She thought she found Orion, the hunter.

The only sounds were the creak of the mast, an occasional flap of the sails and the slap of the waves against the bows. Then Paul said, 'Get below. It's chilly.'

She hadn't noticed him turn before, nor did he now, but he must have known she was here all this while, just behind him.

She almost protested, 'I'm all right, I don't want to go below,' but it was cold, her breath was frosted and she hadn't noticed that before, and he was the skipper and refusing to obey orders could be mutiny.

She looked once more at the stars, at the lights on the swaying mastheads, then she bent down under the hatch coaming and went down the companionway to the main cabin.

The lamps were lit now, and in the galley a coffee pot and a saucepan stood on the hanging calor gas stove. In spite of the movement of the boat the stove stayed level, and the table top was fixed in the same way.

Dan was drinking coffee, plates on the table showed that he had just finished his meal. He said, 'Ready for a bite to eat, then?'

'Oh, please!' She was suddenly ravenous, and he brought her a bowl of thick stew, the dishes all fitted into rimmed depressions in the table top, which she ate with a spoon and a hunk of bread. 'Marvellous,' said Jenny.

'My missus makes a lovely drop of broth,' said Dan.

'She certainly does,' Jenny agreed. 'Does Mrs. Blaskie always do the cooking?'

'Bless ee, no. I bring a drop of broth along sometimes, but most times I cook, or the skipper does.'

'I could get the meals,' Jenny offered, but Dan looked

doubtful about that and she realized she had been pushing. She said fervently, 'Thank you for letting me come,
I'm having a wonderful time,' and Dan admitted she had
been no trouble at all up to now.

When Dan went up to take over the steering Paul came
down for his supper. Paul Tremain was a big man, the
spacious rooms of Moidores had always seemed about the
right size for him, but he moved around the small cabin
and the smaller galley with a co-ordinated economy.
Jenny watched as he brought his meal to the table. She
said, 'I've had the best day of my life.'

That was the simple truth. She had never been so care-
free or so happy. The self-consciousness she had always
felt when she was with Paul, particularly since the accident at the mine, had gone.

He said, 'I'm glad you've enjoyed it.'

It was more than enjoyment, it was deeper and more
satisfying. She said, 'You are so lucky to have this boat.'

'I know that.'

'Where did you find her?'

'Lying at anchor off St. Ives. She's old, her paint had
flaked, but her timbers were sound.' As he ate his meal he
explained the work that had been done to make *Mylor*
seaworthy again, and Jenny listened spellbound. It was as
though she had found and fallen in love with the boat
herself, and helped to bring her back to life.

The strong sea air as well as making her hungry had
made her tired, and in the warm little cabin when the
meal was over and Paul had gone back on deck she found
her eyelids getting heavy.

She would have liked to have gone up again herself,
but Paul said goodnight and told her that Dan had fixed
her cabin. He did not want her on deck in darkness, leaning over the side, and very soon when she was left alone
she was yawning.

She went to her cabin through the access doors, and the
wooden bunk was now a comfortable bed, with a foam
rubber mattress and sleeping bag and a couple of spare
blankets folded on the tin trunk.

There was a pressure lamp fitted to a bracket at the

side of the bunk. She'd never used one of those before, but she wasn't calling to ask how to turn it off if she could work it out for herself. She studied it for a while before deciding which screw to turn, and then the light died away, the faint hot paraffin smell dissipating quickly in the fresh sea air.

She lay in the darkness. In spite of the confined space and the rolling of the ship she was completely relaxed and comfortable. With Paul Tremain at the helm, or indeed with Paul Tremain anywhere, nothing much would go wrong. He had that kind of competence and it was always reassuring.

Everything felt right. She listened to the slap of the waves and the hiss of water creaming past the knife-edged bows. She saw the distorted images of stars through the tiny porthole glass, wet with spray, when the ship rolled sufficiently to show the sky.

Vaguely, later, she recognized the rumble of the anchors going down, but there was no apparent change in movement and she did not realize that the *Mylor* was anchored for the night.

Nor did she realize that she had been asleep. She blinked a little, and there were no stars in the sky, just a grey light showing through the little porthole.

She was awake then, instantly fully alive, and it wasn't sea air she could smell. Someone was cooking, she could smell bacon, and she got up and dressed quickly and went up through the hatch on to the deck. The kitchen and the washroom both led off the main cabin below the wheel-house, but the main cabin converted into a bunk room overnight, and no matter how hungry she was she couldn't barge in there without warning.

The ship was still anchored. Wisps of mist blew over the sea. The light was pearly grey and the clouds seemed low. It was another world, like being the only living soul. No voices, just the wind and the sounds of the sea blending with the creaking of the ship.

There was no one in the wheelhouse, the wheel moved gently, slightly, to and fro, anchored in place with straps. The mast, bare of sails, seemed to gyrate.

She stepped carefully to the bows, holding the rail, and stared down the double chain of the anchors into the depths. How deep? she wondered. And what lives down there in those dark green waters?

'Sleep well?' asked Paul, suddenly from behind her.

She jumped. 'You startled me! Yes, thank you, I slept marvellously.'

He joined her at the rail. 'What were you looking at?'

'Just staring down. Hoping for dolphins, or sea witches.'

He smiled. 'I can't hold out much hope of either, but in the meantime breakfast's nearly ready.'

Jenny washed in the little ablutions area; she needed no make-up today, her skin was glowing and her hair when she combed it crackled like mad. She began to croon to herself from the sheer joy of being alive and when she stepped out into the main cabin she went on humming, under her breath, until she realized that Paul was looking at her, then she stopped.

'What is that you're humming?' he asked. She flushed and laughed.

'I don't know, I think I heard it in a shell. It isn't really a song at all, I can't sing. Although I suppose it's Timmy's song. It sends him to sleep when there are storms around.'

Dan came out of the galley carrying a plate of bacon and eggs and sausages. 'Aye,' he said, 'that could be where you heard it,' and he put down the dish on the little table.

The three of them ate breakfast together, no one doing much talking, not because there was any restraint but as though they knew each other so well they didn't need words.

Jenny could hardly believe that this was her first trip. *Mylor* seemed an old friend, as though Jenny had been beside Paul when he first saw the boat riding at anchor, and when he'd turned from that first sight Jenny's had been the eyes he had met and he had asked, 'Well?' and she had said, 'Yes.'

Now Paul was listening. 'The wind's changing,' he announced, and he and Dan disappeared up the companionway ladder to the deck.

She heard the anchors being taken in and the sound of the engine. There was movement as the ship turned, and she got busy with the washing up, enjoying herself finding the places for the crockery and cutlery.

All the time she could hear shouts and footsteps above as the sails were hoisted and the engines stopped, then the motion of the ship changed again as they heeled to the wind.

Dan had clattered down briefly, seen that Jenny was putting things where they should be and grunted, 'Good lass, put your jacket on when you come up,' then gone back.

When she finished she went on deck and the wind was fresher now, with an occasional thin spurt of rain lashing across. Paul was at the wheel and Dan was busy among the rigging. Jenny went over to Dan and asked, 'What are you doing?'

'Checkin' the lashin' on the cleats,' said Dan.

'What's a cleat?' It was a strange tongue, but Dan pointed out and explained, and when Jenny asked, 'Do you mind if I watch you?' he said,

'Bless ee, m'dear, I don't mind,' so she trotted along behind Dan and got her first lesson in seamanship from an expert.

Paul stayed at the wheel. Later she brought him hot coffee from the galley in a brown enamel jug. Dan had said, 'Take this to the skipper,' and she smiled as she handed it over.

'Tomorrow when I fetch your coffee in the office I'm not going to believe this.'

He agreed, 'It is another life.'

In Tremain he was unapproachable, but here and now she could say, 'Dan says you never really want to go back.'

'I don't.'

She didn't ask, 'Then why do you?' Paul Tremain was Tremain, he had to be in charge or the empire would crumble. She held her own mug of coffee in both hands, letting it warm her fingers, and she said, 'Why did you change Tremain? Why didn't you leave it a sleepy little fishing village?'

'Because it wasn't sleeping, it was dying.'

'*Dying?*'

'Another year or two and it would have been derelict. There isn't enough fish left to provide a livelihood for more than a handful of men. The mine hadn't been worked in generations, the farms weren't being run economically.'

'But why?'

He smiled wryly. 'Because my father was a man who couldn't say no. Everybody liked him. He lived the easy life and it wasn't until he died that I found out Tremain was bankrupt.'

'When it became your responsibility?'

'Yes.'

'What did you want to do with your life?' Although he did the job superbly he had not wanted to be Tremain of Tremain.

'I was going into the Navy, but I came down from university for his funeral and I never went back again.'

'*Why?*' Of course she knew why. Being the man he was he could have made no other choice. He said, mocking himself:

'Because I couldn't leave it to die.'

What had Ebby said when Jenny first came ... 'He won't let any of us down, he'll bear the load.'

Jenny said, 'But you have *Mylor*.' He got his strength renewed from the lonely hours of sailing, and she was only now realizing the extent of her intrusion. She said, 'Thank you for letting me come.'

He smiled and drank his coffee, set the mug down and then said, 'You wanted to come.'

'So very much.'

'Look.' He seized her arm. 'Just off the port bow.' A faint grey shape was rising out of the sea ahead of them and she whispered,

'The Witch's Rock?'

'Yes.'

She had never seen it before from the seaward side. The low mist around it made it look unreal, something from a ghost story, but as they drew nearer she saw that it rose sheer and high surrounded by jagged rocks and crashing waves.

On the day Jenny had picnicked here, coming out from Tremain, the sea had been calm as a millpond, but now the roar of the waves on the rocks was terrifying. She wailed, 'We can't anchor!' and *Mylor* heeled hard over, speeding around the Rock.

Everything happened so quickly. The sails came down as if by magic as the engine started up. Paul swung the wheel violently, first one way and then the other, and the ship passed between two rows of projecting rocks and they were dropping anchor in the tiny bay facing Tremain.

The shelving beach was only a few yards of deep water away, and here was protection from the wind. Jenny was still speechless as Paul picked up a haversack, and the men unlashed the dinghy and threw it overboard.

'I be tellin' av ee, ee'll do this once too often,' said Dan, grinning broadly. Paul grinned too, and Jenny looked at the rise of rock from the little beach and the entrance to the caves.

It was how she remembered, the only difference that between July and November. She was the first to scramble ashore and she helped the men pull the dinghy up on to the beach.

At first the air was full of beating wings, the Rock was a bird sanctuary and they were rarely disturbed, but they settled again, and Dan lit his pipe and sat down on a flat rock puffing contentedly as Paul stood looking out across the water.

Jenny asked, 'Would you have a torch in that haversack?'

'Yes,' said Paul, and she held out a hand for it, explaining:

'I want to look round the caves.'

'Not alone.' As Paul turned to walk over the shingle towards the caves entrance she fell into step beside him.

143

'I went alone last time.'

'When was the last time?'

'The only time. The first year I came here. We came out for a picnic.' Jenny and her mother, Caterine and Lorraine, and one or two others. Not Paul. She only vaguely remembered the others, they were Caterine's friends, it was their yacht. She said, 'It was a blazing hot day, and everyone sunbathed and I went to explore the caves.'

She had stepped into the entrance then as she did now. It was a cool gloom, not entirely dark, with a greenish tinge. Light came in from several fissures and water cascaded down inside from crevices in the rock. Then, as Paul had just done, she had switched on her torch and the smooth coloured pebbles underfoot had shone like jewels and the shells had gleamed pearl-like.

She walked ahead through a string of similar caves with linking passages, straight on, although sometime she would like to explore the narrower passages that ran off this one.

It was all as she remembered, the veined colours of the rock, the natural bridge that took them over running water, and then at last the cavern where everything seemed silver.

The moss was luminous here, you could see without torchlight. There were shining white pillars and water dripping with a sound of tinkling bells. And in the middle the smooth deep pool.

It was just the same. She knelt down to look at her reflection, as she had done as a young girl. It had been the only mirror that made her beautiful, and again her face swam palely with a secret smile. But this time of course there was another reflection, Paul's dark face, dark hair, dark eyes.

It was strange. Of course she knew he was standing behind her, but her first reaction was shock; followed by a turmoil of emotions as though this was the reflection of a stranger and at the same time the one of whom she knew everything.

When she raised her head to turn and look up at him

Paul was not smiling. Their eyes met and locked as he held out a hand. She heard the sea and saw the glittering walls of the silver cave and looked up silently at the man, and it was like something half-recalled from a dream.

Then she took his hand, but she still held back resisting. For seconds, no longer, but time was suddenly unsure. She trembled as she stood against him and his arms tightened around her. They stood utterly still, searching each other's faces in the pale silver light, and to Jenny recognition came.

She saw her own dark lover. No other woman's, as she could be no other man's. Deep calling deep, as though they had been together through ages past and nothing could ever part them for more than a moment.

Paul still held her and looked at her, and someone was shouting from somewhere.

The shout broke the spell. It was Dan hollering 'Skipper!' sounding as though he called through cupped hands through the echoing caverns.

'What is it?' Paul shouted back. He picked up the kit bag and torch, slung the kit bag over his shoulder and kept a guiding arm around Jenny.

Dan was easy to find. He was in the central passage and he came towards the gleam of their torch. He said as he neared them, 'I'm not over fond of the looks of this ole sky. Unless we belong to stay here for the night we best be casting off.'

'Right,' said Paul. 'Come on, Jenny.'

They went quickly and the sky was overcast. Jenny blinked as they came out on to the shingle; it looked later than she had expected, they must have been in the caves an hour or more, it hadn't seemed so long. Dan, a little ahead, had already begun to drag the dinghy into the water.

As the engines of *Mylor* started up the seagulls flew again, wildly for a few minutes. Paul was at the wheel and Jenny stood at the rail, watching the lights coming on in Tremain.

It might have been the atmosphere of the Rock, and remembering the old legend that had stirred Jenny so strangely, but that didn't change the fact that as surely as the sea was in her blood so was Paul Tremain. The wind and the spray stung against her skin, and there was nothing dreamlike about it, it was stinging sharp and bitter cold.

She was awake and thinking clearly, and she knew that she wanted Paul to make love to her, to love her, to need her as lover and friend and companion and sharer in everything for ever.

That was how he had looked at her in the caves, but who had he seen in that brief moment? Jenny or Caterine?

She must have looked like Caterine, hair loose in the faint silver light; they all said she looked like Caterine. And when the spell broke Paul had turned back at once into skipper, intent on getting his boat safely back into harbour, a hundred per cent practical and competent, as though for him that moment had been for a memory not for the flesh-and-blood girl who was still beside him.

The waves were high, threatening to break over the decks, and he called now, 'Get below, Jenny!'

'We're nearly in Tremain.' She came to the comparative shelter of the wheelhouse. It was a turbulent sea, but there had been no thunder or lightning and she hoped that Timmy was safely home. Out at sea she had forgotten the problems in Tremain for a while, but now she remembered Lorraine and Rolf and said, 'You see things clearer from here.'

'I've found that,' said Paul.

'You wouldn't dismiss Rolf and cut Lorraine off if they married.' She knew that for certain now.

'No,' said Paul, 'but if the risk stops them they're not very involved.'

'Rolf would chance it.'

Paul's voice was dry. 'I'm more concerned about Lorraine.'

The storm didn't develop, although the winds continued to lash the sea and were something to battle against on the way along the cliff top road back to Moidores.

Paul took the brunt, with Jenny hanging on to his arm, with no breath for words or laughter, although it was a little comic, and they smiled at each other more than once when Jenny almost spun off her feet, or when a particularly strong and steady gust took all their weight to stay where they were.

Once in the house Paul went into the study, checking if anything untoward had happened in his absence, and Jenny went seeking Timmy and Lorraine.

They were in the drawing room in front of a blazing fire. 'You went *sailing*?' Lorraine squeaked.

'It was wonderful.' Jenny described the trip mainly for Timmy, whose eyes widened fearfully when she said they had moored a while at the Witch's Rock.

But Jenny's own delight was contagious, the little bridge, the silver cave that played music . . . the strange cave, although she didn't say that, where she had known that she belonged to Paul Tremain. . . .

Timmy had been to the Rock in summertime. 'Yeah,' he said now, remembering pleasant hours, 'it's a smashing place.'

It had also been a smashing party. He had won a trumpet, and brought home a piece of cake for Jenny, and when he went up to bed he played his trumpet all the way. He seemed in high spirits, but when he put down his trumpet on the formica-top under the window he said thoughtfully, 'Auntie Jen, I know Mom had a car smash, I know that's what happened. It wasn't the sea, or anything's fault.'

'No, love,' said Jenny gently.

'She has gone, hasn't she?'

'Yes, Timmy.'

'She isn't in her room.' He watched Jenny closely. 'The door's always locked, but she isn't in there, is she?'

'No,' said Jenny, 'there's nothing in there but furniture and clothes. It's just an empty room.'

The door had to be opened so that Timmy could see that, and Ebby promised, 'I'll have a word with Mr. Paul,' when Jenny told her.

Lorraine said fiercely, 'I think Caterine's things should

147

be left where they are.'

'We'll see what Mr. Paul says,' said Ebby.

Next morning Paul handed over the key to the house-keeper and Ebby went in to take off the dust sheets and give the room an airing and a cleaning.

It was an ordinary Monday morning in the office, but not for Jenny. When she brought in mid-morning coffee she knew Paul was reminded of yesterday, and she could taste salt spray on her own lips. There was a complicity between them. She had an understanding of him now that few others had.

At midday Paul went off to the home farm, he and the manager were going somewhere to buy a tractor. Mr. Morrison was spending the afternoon working on the accounts, and over lunch Ebby suggested that Jenny and Lorraine might look through Caterine's clothes.

'Mr. Paul said to give them away, or send them to a charity. It's a wicked waste to leave them hanging in the cupboards and filling the drawers.'

That was a task neither girl wanted. Caterine's perfume was everywhere when they stirred the silks of lingerie drawers and opened the wardrobe again. But it was wasteful to leave such beautiful and expensive clothes to the moths.

Jenny could have worn most of them, but they would have given her no pleasure, they were gorgeous but they were still poignantly Caterine's, and Lorraine was too tall and too pale.

Ebby would know how to dispose of them, and Jenny and Lorraine emptied the drawers, making tidy heart-breaking piles of Caterine's things.

They took the dresses and the suits and the coats with the couture name-tabs from the hangers, and Lorraine would say, 'She only bought this the week before,' or, 'She looked lovely in this.'

They were taking out shoes, dozens of pairs, when Lorraine picked up a slip of paper from the back of the closet. They had emptied drawers and cupboards of trivia as they had gone along, putting most of it into the waste-paper basket.

Lorraine read this, and gasped as she read.

'What is it?' Jenny took it from her nerveless fingers, and her own eyes raced over the lines in outraged disbelief. 'This isn't *true*! It *can't* be!'

It was a page of a letter. Passionate and pleading. Begging 'Caterina' to leave Paul Tremain.

CHAPTER EIGHT

LORRAINE said in a small stunned voice, 'It's from Rolf.' It was typewritten and there seemed no proof who had typed it.

Jenny was stunned herself. Her own voice was a whisper. 'It isn't true, Caterine couldn't—'

'Oh, but she could. Because he was mine. She could think that was the joke.'

'Of course it's not Rolf.'

'That was our meeting place.' It mentioned Purdie's Beck, and Lorraine's smooth face was white and lined as though she was in pain.

'Rolf loves you,' Jenny insisted. 'On Saturday he said it's always been up to you,' but Lorraine was listening to nothing but her own thoughts.

'I knew she could have anyone she wanted, but I never thought she'd dare cheat on Paul. He could give her more than anyone else, and that was what counted with Caterine: money, position. It *was*!' She sounded as though she expected Jenny to deny it, and Jenny crumpled the letter fiercely.

This was no nonsense thing, this was a physical affair. 'Paul mustn't know,' Jenny said.

'How *could* Rolf?'

Rolf was Lorraine's problem, Jenny was protecting her own. She caught Lorraine's arm, making her listen. 'You're not to tell Paul. Caterine's dead. No one's going to spoil her memory.'

'*Tell Paul?*' Lorraine echoed shrilly. 'Can you see me?'

Jenny couldn't, but she could see that jealousy had prised Lorraine's shallowness and gone deep. Perhaps that was where Rolf had made his mistake, he had been too available, Lorraine had believed she could turn to him this-year-next-year. 'No,' she had told Jenny, 'Rolf hasn't found anyone else.' Now she would never be so smugly confident again.

Jenny did not believe for a moment that it was Rolf Perrie, but she said, 'If you're jealous ask him. Although you've no grounds for complaining, you opted out. And why should he wait for ever, he's an attractive man?'

But not to Jenny, and how could Paul's wife want any other man? She opened her hand on the crushed letter and the enormity of it overwhelmed her again. 'This – isn't Caterine.'

'How do you know?' Lorraine sounded bitter. 'You haven't lived with her for the last eight years. She could charm the birds off the trees, but she wanted everything.'

They had gone through pockets, but casually, not as searchers, and now Jenny turned again to the piles of clothes. Paul mustn't know. There must be nothing left to start a wildfire of scandal when Caterine's possessions were handled around in Tremain, or wherever Ebby was sending them. Jenny was going through everything again with a fine toothcomb, looking for any scrap of evidence.

Not that she cared who had sent the letter. She didn't want to find any more evidence, the prospect horrified her. She went through the pockets of the first jacket and checked in the lining and Lorraine said quite calmly, 'I can't. I've seen enough.'

'I must,' said Jenny.

Lorraine pressed her fingertips to her temples. 'I think I'm going to have the migraine of my life, and when it's over I'll go and see Rolf. I'm sorry I can't help you any more.'

'There's no need,' said Jenny, remembering Caterine's little writing bureau downstairs, her diary, wondering was there anywhere else that secrets might hide. She was sure there was no local gossip, she would have heard a whisper of it if there had been.

Lorraine went slowly to the door. She began, 'If you find anything else—'

'I shall burn it,' said Jenny.

'That would be the best thing,' said Lorraine.

Jenny searched like a crime-squad member for clues. She went with quick deft fingers through everything in that room, even the junk in the wastepaper basket was now suspect: theatre tickets, meal checks, hotel receipts. She burned them on the open fires downstairs, some in this room, some in that. The mass of papers in the bureau seemed innocuous and the desk diary had always been open for anyone to see, full of social engagements but nothing that looked like code or incrimination.

Caterine had covered her wandering tracks well. The only betrayal was that single sheet.

Lorraine had gone to bed and Ebby was blaming herself for the migraine. 'A bit too much for her, going though the mistress's things.' She looked with concern at Jenny. 'Not a nice job for either of you, but it had to be done. Come and have a cup of tea now.'

Jenny was looking strained too, and Ebby resolved to get the contents of that room out tomorrow.

The curtains in Lorraine's room were closed and Jenny opened the door silently and came to the bedside, making no sound on the thick carpet. She would have left again without speaking if Lorraine hadn't asked, 'Did you find anything?'

'No. How's the head?'

'Horrible,' said Lorraine weakly.

'I'm sorry.' The migraine was real enough, but it was also an escape, as Lorraine's not-too-robust physique always seemed to provide an escape from harsh reality. Jenny said, 'Try to rest.'

'I will. A night's sleep should settle it.'

'What about tomorrow?' Jenny couldn't help asking, and Lorraine's pain-filled eyes looked at her steadily.

'Tomorrow I grow up,' said Lorraine.

There was just Paul and Timmy and Jenny for dinner that evening, and Timmy had been thinking during the day about Jenny having gone sailing on the *Mylor*. She had enjoyed herself so much and he believed what she told him so implicitly that his nameless fears had disappeared.

Sometimes he thought he would like to go sailing again himself. He would be safe with his father, he always knew that, but if Auntie Jen was going they would have a lot of fun. Timothy worshipped his father, but his father was never scared, you couldn't tell him that storms made you feel sick unless Auntie Jen sang to you. Not as badly as they used to, but out at sea they might.

There was nothing you could teach Father or show him that he didn't know already, but you had to take care of Auntie Jen sometimes, and she tucked you in better at night and she had soft hands.

Timothy asked over the soup, 'Auntie Jen will be coming, won't she?'

Timothy's presence seemed conditional on that and Jenny was relieved when Paul smiled and said, 'I hope she will, you'd better ask her.'

Jenny and Timothy began to plan long journeys, taking in all sorts of impossible places, and ending almost seriously with a globe of the world and a huge atlas, brought into the drawing-room from the library and plonked on the floor.

Paul sat in a leather wing-backed chair, but Jenny and Timothy knelt beside the globe. Whether they would ever sail to the Greek Islands Jenny couldn't know, but the thought of it filled her with delight. Paul seemed to consider it possible; he described the wonders, answering Timmy's questions, and Jenny found that she was listening to him as saucer-eyed as Timothy. She grimaced to herself ruefully. She didn't want to pass as another child, least of all with Paul.

Lorraine didn't come down that evening, she was sleeping when Jenny peeped in again after she had put Timmy to bed.

Downstairs Paul was turning the globe reflectively, and Jenny went back to her patch on the carpet, the other side of the globe, and asked, 'Was that make-believe for Timmy, about taking the *Mylor* to Greece?'

'Not entirely. It's a trip I've thought about for when I can find the time.'

'Why don't you make the time?'

He smiled, 'It might come to that.' He didn't take many holidays. Caterine had always been going on a jet-plane to somewhere. She had had fabulous holidays with friends, with Lorraine and Timmy, but Paul had usually been too busy to join them.

Perhaps he had neglected her, not materially, heaven knows, but perhaps that explained the note they had found this afternoon. It was burnt now, gone, and Paul was never going to know if Jenny could help it. If his pride wouldn't let Caterine take the small T.V. parts she had been offered from time to time how would he react to learning she had taken a lover?

'Who are you protecting at Moidores, the child or the man?' Jack Bastaple had sneered. Right now – the man. Strong though he was, Jenny was his shield in this.

She touched the globe. 'So tell me again where we're going,' and they went over the route again, and then over countless seas to numberless countries. They twirled the world on its axis, and Jenny asked, 'You'll take me with you?'

'Of course.'

'If you don't I'll swim after you.'

He smiled, 'I'm beginning to believe that!'

'I was going to. I had my shoes off and my coat and I was nearly out of my skirt. It was as well you were rowing and had your back to the jetty and I had time to get into them again. The children were fascinated and Grace Norwood was in hysterics.'

He was laughing when Ebby tapped the slightly open door and stepped in to say Mr. Morrison was on the phone. She stayed to look wonderingly after him. 'I haven't heard Mr. Paul laugh like that since I don't know when.'

'Since – Caterine died?' But Ebby shook her head,

'Since his father died, more like.'

'What was his father like, Ebby? Everybody seems to have been very fond of him.'

Ebby's smile was fond too. 'Ah, you'd have liked him. He was a real gentleman.'

'So they all say,' Jenny teased. 'Meaning that Paul isn't,'

and Ebby turned on her indignantly.

'I mean nothing of the sort – of course Mr. Paul's a gentleman. And he's twice the man his father was, which is as well for all of us if not for him. He works too hard.'

'He is thinking about a holiday some time,' Jenny ventured. 'Sailing to the Greek Islands, taking Timmy and me.'

She wondered how Ebby would take that. She hadn't said much about Jenny's last brief trip, and she was somewhat straitlaced, and setting off for a month or two in the *Mylor* might bring out her strong disapproval.

But Ebby showed no surprise at all. She said, 'Dan Blaskie was telling his wife the skipper wouldn't be sailing alone again,' and while Jenny was assimilating that she smiled. . . .

Lorraine was over the worst of her migraine by morning. She was pale at breakfast and she told them she was going over to the Perries'. Paul took no particular notice, but he caught Jenny's questioning glance, quickly though she tried to mask it.

Before she went into the office Jenny managed a few moments alone with Lorraine and warned her, 'If the letter wasn't from Rolf you realize you could be starting up a scandal?'

'I can't help that.'

'Mrs. Perrie dislikes Paul. If she gets to hear everyone else will.'

'Rolf wouldn't tell her.'

'Maybe not, if he was the man. If he wasn't he very well might, or at any rate discuss it with his father.'

'I've got to know,' insisted Lorraine.

They were still at the breakfast table. Lorraine had eaten nothing and only drunk half a cup of coffee. 'Why?' said Jenny levelly. 'What right have you?'

'You don't understand.' That was a snub to shut Jenny up, and Lorraine pushed back her chair, but Jenny was at the door first.

'Please,' Jenny begged, 'ask him if you must, but please don't say we found a letter. Just say you're jealous, you're scared there might have been someone.'

Lorraine smiled bleakly. 'That's what it comes down to, doesn't it? I'm jealous and I'm scared – and how can I start to tell him that?'

'You could start by telling him you love him,' said Jenny.

'Yes,' Lorraine sounded as though that had occurred to her, 'I could, couldn't I?'

Lorraine was back at Moidores for lunch, but Jenny had lunch in the office. Paul had a full list of appointments and Mr. Morrison was working like a beaver. Most of the exterior property repairs and painting in Tremain was done during the winter months, and it seemed that every building has a list of 'musts'. It was after six o'clock before Jenny could get to Lorraine.

She was desperately anxious to know what had happened and for once in her life she could have done without Timmy's chatter. Lorraine wasn't going out of her way to tell. There always seemed to be someone else within earshot, Ebby, Dolly and Timothy at first, and then Paul. As though Lorraine was deliberately avoiding being alone with Jenny.

That wasn't encouraging; Jenny had to read what she could without being told. Lorraine was quiet and appeared thoughtful. Thoughtful or depressed, it was hard to tell.

When Paul asked after Rolf she said, 'He's fine – he's back at work on Monday, isn't he?'

Paul said that he was and that was all that was said about Rolf, but Jenny noticed that Lorraine didn't look at Paul when she spoke to him. She kept her eyes downcast, and then perhaps Jenny's anxiety communicated itself, because she gave Jenny a half smile.

After saying good night to Timmy Jenny went back again into Caterine's room. The scent still lingered, it was taking the clothes from the cupboards. It could still bring back the memory of Caterine so vividly that Jenny could almost see her.

It was hard for Jenny to believe in that letter even now, but Lorraine had believed it. 'Caterine wanted everything. . . . You haven't lived with her for the past eight years,' Lorraine had said. Nor for the three years before her marriage either. Caterine had been Jenny's dream sister and of course there were things Jenny didn't know, but she loved her and mourned her and felt older than Caterine now, as though Caterine had been a beautiful wilful child who must be protected. If Jenny had found that letter when she was alone she would have burned it and no one would have seen it.

. . . 'That was what counted with Caterine, money, position,' . . . 'Caterine never wanted anything except a bigger bracelet.' . . . Jenny stroked the silk dress on top of the pile of dresses. She hadn't realized that she could feel sorry for Caterine. Not the searing sorrow that had come with Caterine's death, but a quiet regret that Caterine should have cared so much for the things that hardly mattered at all.

Lorraine held the bracelet. She was sitting in the drawing-room, where Jenny had left her to go upstairs with Timmy, and she was holding the bracelet from the painting. Jack Bastaple had painted two bracelets as golden chains, and the other bracelet was on the table.

There was a large white leather jewellery box and several flat boxes, and one of the paintings was down, revealing the wall safe behind.

All Caterine's belongings had come to Paul. They had made wills when they married, his providing for a host of dependants – Caterine's share would have made her a wealthy widow – she willing her nothing to him. Eight years later she had left a sizeable bank account and some enviable jewellery. Today he had collected the jewellery from the bank vaults and taken out the pieces that had been left in the wall safe.

He said, 'I think Caterine would have wanted you to share this.'

Lorraine and Jenny, her sisters. Lorraine held the bracelet on the flat of her hand and said in an unnaturally high voice, 'I think she would rather have been buried with it.' And then, 'Oh no! Oh, I'm sorry,' looking wildly and piteously from Paul to Jenny.

Paul said harshly, 'Perhaps you'll decide what you want. I'll leave you to it.'

He went and Lorraine dropped her hands into her lap, and the heavy bracelet fell to the floor. She whispered, 'Why did I say that?'

'Because you think Caterine could have taken Rolf, I suppose,' said Jenny with anger.

'I don't think it was Rolf.'

'You told him about the letter?'

'No.' Because of that Jenny would forgive her most things. 'I had no right, like you said. But that doesn't stop me being scared when I realize I could have lost him. He still loves me.' That seemed to surprise her. 'Caterine called him a ploughboy and said I'd be a fool to marry him.' She picked up Caterine's bracelet and put it on the table. 'I think he'll be a fool to marry me because I am such a coward, but I do love him.'

'I'm glad,' said Jenny. 'Why didn't you tell me?'

'I wanted to run away.' Lorraine was shamefaced although she was smiling. 'That was my idea. Paul could still have sacked Rolf and thrown his folk off their farm, but he couldn't have unmarried us and that was what I wanted to do, only Rolf wasn't having it.'

She was regretful as though she would still have preferred that way. 'Rolf says we have to tell Paul what we're doing.'

You face Paul and you face reality, thought Jenny. You could have the price you'll have to pay spelled out for you. She could have told Lorraine there would be no backlash, but she mustn't.

She asked again, 'Why didn't you tell me this before?' and Lorraine got up and hugged her.

'Because you're not a coward. You're going to say – all right, tell Paul, what are you waiting for? And I'm waiting for Thursday.'

'Thursday?' Jenny echoed. 'What's special about Thursday?'

'Rolf said take another day or two to be sure. He'll come here on Thursday and ask me again. And then we'll tell Paul.'

'Are you sure?'

'Oh yes.' For the first time there was ringing sincerity in Lorraine's voice. 'But I'd give my right hand to know that Paul won't make it hard on the Perries and won't sack Rolf.'

'I've never thought he would,' said Jenny, and Lorraine grabbed that as though it was eighteen-carat reassurance.

'You haven't, have you, and you're pretty close to Paul, aren't you?' To change the subject, with the risk that she wouldn't be able to resist saying, 'I know it will be all right because Paul told me,' Jenny turned to the jewellery and said wryly,

'You've got a dowry here whatever happens, and you're welcome to the lot. I don't want any.'

'Because of what I just said? Oh, Jenny, I'm sorry, of course Caterine would have wanted us to have them. That was sheer bitchiness.'

Caterine had been generous. She had always brought presents when she came home. Of course none of the gifts had meant any sacrifice, she had given away nothing she wanted herself, and Lorraine probably knew more than Jenny how possessive she was over her jewellery.

But Caterine didn't want it now, and no woman could have been unmoved by the beauty of stones and workmanship. These were exquisite pieces, every one. Caterine had always had good taste, and these were heirlooms for the future.

'Please,' said Lorraine. 'The bracelets, you should have those – they're heavy, they'll suit you better.' She looked around, anxious to involve Jenny. 'There's a silver and pearl filigree set here that I've always liked.' She found the box and opened it. 'You know, I've never had much fun wearing jewellery before because Caterine always looked so much better than I did in everything.'

She took out the necklace, which was fine as a frozen spider's web, and held it against Jenny's throat and the scarlet sweater she was wearing. A red jumper was hardly right, but Lorraine said, 'So do you. You could stand here if this room was full and almost everyone would be watching you, but it wouldn't hurt.'

She was looking at the jewels, remembering Caterine wearing them and the years of living as Caterine's shadow. 'Because you wouldn't be laughing at me, would you?'

Jenny protested, 'I don't believe that Caterine was laughing at you,' and Lorraine tried to laugh at herself.

'She laughed at most things.'

'Yes, she did.' Life had been gay and good for Caterine, what did she know of bruised egos? and Lorraine was easier bruised than most.

Lorraine was a baby when her mother died, only a child when she lost her father. From then on her brother had been an autocratic father-like figure, less approachable than her real father had been. She still held him in awe. Caterine had dazzled her, and outshone her in everything.

After Thursday when she knew that Paul would put no obstacles in the way of her marrying Rolf, and when she had proved her own courage to herself by defying Paul, she could well bloom wonderfully.

Jenny, although her heart was hardly in it, sat down with her and chose some pieces of Caterine's jewellery, and helped Lorraine choose. Trying them on, comparing and admiring, as though they were dipping into the junk jewellery in the little shop down in the harbour rather than sharing out a small fortune.

When they finished Jenny got up. 'Where are you going?' Lorraine asked.

'To find Paul.'

'You wouldn't tell him, would you? I promised Rolf I wouldn't get you to tell him.'

'I'm glad about that,' said Jenny.

'You promise?'

'Like a flash.'

'I think I'll take mine to my room.' Lorraine gathered them together in the larger jewel box, and Jenny said doubtfully:

'Do you think it's safe? If you mislay any of that there's going to be trouble.'

'If Paul puts them in the wall safe he might not let me have them back again. They are a gift, aren't they? He has given them to me.'

'Yes,' Jenny agreed. 'And he couldn't have timed it better.'

Lorraine smiled impishly. 'I don't know whether I'm so happy I could cry, or so scared I could cry.'

'But you and Rolf are getting married?'

'Yes.' Her eyes shone like sapphires. 'I'm scared of facing Paul, but oh, Jenny, I am happy!'

Jenny found Paul in the office, sitting at his desk, with the documents Mr. Morrison had left for him. She said, 'Please would you come and put this back in the safe?'

'Have you shared it?'

'Yes.'

He walked with her to the drawing-room and asked, 'Where's Lorraine?'

'She's gone to her room.'

Obviously taking her share with her. Paul looked quizzically at Jenny and she found herself blushing as though she had a guilty secret. It was remembering what she had said about a dowry. Because she knew why Lorraine feared that Paul might regret and possibly revoke his generosity.

He picked up the jewel cases left on the table. 'You want it all put away?' She nodded. 'Then you'd better learn the combination.'

She tried to explain, 'I would be happier with just one piece, I don't really want—' but he overrode that impatiently.

'This is Caterine's gift to you, not mine. This puts you under no obligation to me.'

She bit her lip on a smile. 'You mean I can put them into a suitcase and ring for a taxi?'

'If you like.' With his back to her he began to open the safe and she began to laugh. He asked, 'Is that amusing?'

'Yes.' Ridiculous and impossible. She said, 'I don't ever want to leave here, unless I can come right back.' He turned then and smiled and said:

'Come and see how this works.'

She watched and memorized, and when he put back the portrait of a fair-haired girl who looked a little like Lorraine, painted in the year Victoria became queen, she said, 'Don't work any more tonight. I can tell you what's in that pile on your desk. Mr. Morrison dictated it to me and I typed it. Twenty-two roofs need repairing for a start and they won't get repaired tonight, so that can wait till morning.'

'How bad are the roofs?'

'A tile off here and there.'

'That can wait till morning.' He took her hand and drew her down beside him on the settee in front of the fire. He said, 'When you leave I'll take you, to make sure you come back.'

'Do you want me to tell you about the work on your desk?'

'No, I want you to stay here with me, and be quiet.'

She slid inside his arms and laid her head on his chest, and she felt him relax. After a while she said quietly, 'Was it a grim day?'

'Like most of them.'

'Nothing you couldn't handle?'

'That's the size of it.'

He could handle all the emergencies, all the strains and the stresses. He had the strength and the self-discipline and the brains and the guts, but last night and tonight he had come home to her. And if she had felt relaxed and safe in her berth on the *Mylor* with Paul at the wheel she was infinitely more content now, half asleep in his arms, watching the fire flare and flicker, listening to the sea.

They talked lazily when they talked at all, easy as old friends, and when a clock chimed midnight Jenny said, 'I'd better get to my bed, I'd better say good night,' and moved her head to touch Paul's cheek with her lips.

His skin was not quite smooth and he turned so that their mouths brushed, and kissed her briefly but with a purpose and feeling that every nerve in her answered. Then he said huskily, 'I think you had. Good night, Jenny. Bless you.'

She said good night. Timmy was sleeping. Jenny slept too, and Paul stayed with her in her dreams.

Next afternoon Jenny was out of the office, down in Tremain with Mr. Morrison still dealing with repairs and renovations. The shop was shut and there was no sign of Lorraine, and when they finished, and Mr. Morrison went home to his rooms in the Crow's Nest pub half-way up the hill, Jenny looked in on Grace Norwood.

She hadn't seen Grace since Saturday, when she had left her laughing on the quayside, and Grace's first words were, 'You're staying to eat, aren't you?'

'Thanks,' said Jenny.

She went to phone from the shop to tell Ebby she wouldn't be very late, and had a word with Timmy, then she took Grace the spare key back and helped to lay the table.

Ben's latest masterpiece was set in the centre of the table; he had brought it over from the studio that afternoon. It was a hideously scowling head in grey granite, and as she laid the plates around it Jenny patted the head and said, 'Hello.'

'Like him?' asked Grace.

'I don't know that I'd care to live with him,' said Jenny.

'I hope somebody will,' laughed Grace. 'We need the money.' Ben's powerful studies sold well. The uglier they were the quicker they sold.

He looked up from his armchair and his newspaper now and asked, 'Don't you recognize Paul Tremain?'

'You've got to be joking!' Jenny exploded. 'This is one of your old Cornish giants.'

'Isn't Paul Tremain?' Ben grinned at her.

'Well, he doesn't look like that,' said Jenny. 'You look more like that than he does. Go on, frown and twist your mouth to one side.' As he obliged she pointed a fork at him. 'That's it! It's a self-portrait. They've all been self-portraits. Grace, you're married to a Cornish monster.'

'I've suspected it for a long time,' gurgled Grace.

The Norwoods ate heartily, they enjoyed their food, and tonight's meal was a steak-and-kidney pie, cauliflower au gratin, and a bottle of red wine in Jenny's honour. Eating and talking passed a pleasant hour or so.

There were two subjects intriguing Grace: Jenny's trip in the *Mylor* and Caterine's jewellery.

Jenny described the route the *Mylor* had taken, and said she had had a marvellous time, and Grace seemed almost as pleased to hear about the sharing of the jewellery as though she had been included herself.

Lorraine had told them about that this morning. 'I suppose it was the obvious thing for him to do,' said Grace. 'You are Caterine's family, after all. Which is your favourite?'

'I don't know,' Jenny admitted, and Grace began enthusing about the piece she coveted most, the silver filigree that had been Lorraine's first choice.

Lorraine had told them about the jewellery, but she hadn't told them she and Rolf were planning to get married. If she had Grace would have had some questions to ask about that. Jenny said nothing, although when Grace did hear she was going to be indignant. 'You *knew*, Jenny, and you never breathed a word?' But Jenny had promised and it wouldn't be long before everyone knew.

She helped with the washing-up and refused to let either Ben or both of them walk to Moidores with her. The offers were kindly, but of course they would rather stay by their cosy fireside, and Jenny would walk fast and she had no fears here.

When she had gone Grace looked at the carved head again and asked her husband, 'That isn't really meant to be Tremain, is it?'

'Good lord, no!' Ben chuckled at his joke. 'But didn't Jenny rise to it?'

The harbour was deserted except for one man, leaning on the sea wall, looking out across the dark waters, and Jenny recognized Jack Bastaple. He said, 'Good evening,' as though he was expecting her.

'Hello.'

'Did you get the bracelets?' He had heard about the jewellery. Lorraine had been down in the shop, so it would have been news for all the artists' colony.

Jenny said, 'Yes,' and Jack walked along beside her.

'And do they feel like chains?'

She turned on him angrily but kept walking. 'They were never chains.' The night was clear, with the usual wind from the sea whipping her hair, and he said raggedly:

'You look more like Caterine every time I see you.'

She was angry, but she pitied him. She asked almost gently, 'Have you painted the picture again?'

'I've tried.' He shrugged heavily. 'But I don't think it's going to work a second time.' He looked out again to sea. The *Mylor* in the mouth of the harbour had a light on its masthead like a star. He said, 'You went sailing. Are you falling for it too?'

'For what?'

'The *Mylor*. Moidores. All of it. Do you want to be Queen of Tremain?'

There was nothing to say to that. She walked on and he still walked beside her, taunting her, 'After Queen Caterina Queen Jenny doesn't sound right, does it?'

Caterina ... the name in the letter. ... And Purdie's Beck when he was painting the old mine entrance. Jack Bastaple had always been much more likely than Rolf Perrie. She asked, 'Is that what you called Caterine – Caterina?'

'Sometimes.' His voice was husky.

'And you tried to get her to leave Paul.' That wasn't a question, but he answered:

'Yes.'

'I see,' she said, and he said, 'You don't.'

But she did, and she could have said, 'You had an affair with Caterine, but it was never serious for her. It would be a joke, because Caterine laughed at everything. A secret joke and no more.' But she said nothing.

He went on, 'She wasted her talents, she wasted her life here. He made her afraid to risk living poor. She couldn't get away.'

'Couldn't or wouldn't?' That Jenny had to say.

'Couldn't,' he said. '*Couldn't*. Tremain would never

have let her go. He keeps what he has, and he was born to it. Everything handed to him on a plate.' Bitterness choked him. He was overwhelmed by envy so that he sounded as though he tasted bile on his tongue, and almost spat out, 'He just sits back and the money rolls in.'

'Nonsense,' said Jenny briskly. 'He works a darn sight harder than you've ever done, my lad.' She realized that she sounded like Ebby. She said, 'Good night,' and left him at the corner of the road that led to his cottage, and went up the hill so fast that she was out of breath before she reached the Crow's Nest and had to slow down and take the rest at a reasonable rate.

Jenny went into Moidores by the kitchen door and Ebby greeted her with, 'You picked the wrong night to stay out, we've been having some real excitement here.'

'What?'

Both Eb and Ebby were smiling, but almost guiltily. 'Seems we're having a wedding,' said Ebby.

Why had they brought the announcement forward? And had they told Paul yet or only Eb and Ebby? Jenny asked, 'Where are they?'

'Gone to tell his folk,' said Eb. 'Even they didn't know.' He fixed Jenny with a shrewd eye. 'You did, though.'

She nodded, then swallowed to ask, 'How did Paul take it?'

'He's eating his dinner,' said Ebby, 'so it hasn't taken his appetite.'

'Good. Are you pleased?'

Eb said firmly, 'Rolf Perrie's a nice young fellow, I never could understand what the master had against him,' and Ebby went on smiling,

'Of course we're pleased. She looked so happy. She said to tell you she'd see you later.'

Paul and Timothy were alone in the dining-room and the meal was almost finished. Timothy was eating the last crumb of chocolate sponge pudding and Paul had cheese and biscuits on his plate. They both looked towards the door, they had heard Jenny coming, but only Timothy was smiling.

Timmy burst out as she walked in, 'Auntie Jen, did you know Auntie Lorraine's getting married?'

'Ebby's just told me,' she said, and Paul's expression conveyed such a grasp of the situation that Jenny couldn't meet his eyes. Timmy babbled on, 'She's marrying Rolf. Isn't that super?'

'Super,' echoed Jenny weakly.

'I like Rolf,' Timmy confided. 'I think that's a good idea.' He scraped his dish and Jenny said:

'Finished? Come on, then.'

Timmy had expected more chat, but Jenny was turning towards the door again, so he said good night to his father and went with her.

Paul did not think it was super. No one had expected he would. But he had looked at Jenny just now as though it was at least partly her fault, and she was not looking forward to being questioned.

'John's coming to tea tomorrow,' Timmy, pyjamaed and ready for bed, reminded her.

'That's nice.' She knew. Children were always coming to tea. Timothy had a sociable little gang of playmates.

'Shall we play with the train set?'

'Why not?'

'Shall we get them out now?' he suggested cunningly. The play was to delay bedtime and Jenny was tempted to agree and stretch out another half hour or so before she went down to Paul again. But Paul had to be faced, and Lorraine was happy, and happiness was surely what Paul really wanted for his sister.

'Get the trains out when John comes tomorrow,' said Jenny. 'You can set them up between you.'

Timmy hadn't thought the ploy would work, although it had been worth trying. He grinned, 'I hate you.'

'I hate you.' Jenny tickled him briefly, and he squirmed and spluttered, and asked when she let him go:

'Will Auntie Lorraine go away?'

'Not far.' Rolf would still be working at the mine.

'But she won't live in this house any more?'

So far as space went there would be plenty of room for a flat. But space might not be the problem.

'I don't know. Into bed with you.' Timmy clambered into his bunk and she said, 'Good night, love.'

She didn't have to stay around until he fell asleep now. He was well through the stage of utter dependence on her. He was a healthy happy small boy again, the nightmares fading.

Paul was still sitting at the dining-room table, and Jenny went back into the room. The sooner this was over the better. He looked weary, but he looked grim too, and although she had intended to say, 'Please don't be angry,' she sat down before she tried to start explaining and he spoke first.

'You knew they planned to get married?'

'Yes.'

'Why didn't you tell me?'

'I – promised not to say anything.'

'It seems I should have asked for your promise instead of relying on your discretion.'

He thought she hold told them that Rolf's career was not in jeopardy, and that Paul was not going to finish with Lorraine if she married against his wishes. Well, she had always said she believed that.

She demanded, 'What does it matter? What have you got against Rolf?'

'Nothing,' said Paul, 'but I should like to have been sure that Lorraine's attraction for him wasn't the mine and the money.'

Put starkly like that it was horrifying. Jenny was so shaken that she was almost incoherent. 'Why should it be? Rolf is in love with her. How can you think he only wants her because—' Words failed her. It was degrading to say them. But Paul said quietly:

'Why not? That was why Caterine married me.'

Power was overwhelmingly attractive to some women, and Paul Tremain's empire would have made him outstandingly eligible, but Jenny stammered, 'Caterine loved you.'

'Less than she loved what I could buy for her. I realized that very soon.' He spoke calmly and his smile was self-mocking. 'It didn't affect me too deeply, but Lorraine is a different proposition.' He stopped smiling and said harshly, 'It could destroy her.'

'Not Rolf.' He had to believe that. 'I'm sure, I'm *sure.*'

He said flatly, 'We'll never be sure now.'

But Jenny knew that Rolf had always been prepared to risk everything for Lorraine. He would have loved her if she had been a salesgirl in the little shop in the harbour, instead of Tremain's sister, the golden girl. She had to make Paul understand. She said, 'Rolf told me last week – "It's up to Lorraine. It's always been up to Lorraine".'

He believed her so far. He said cynically, 'Then you told Lorraine I was bluffing and she told Rolf?'

'I *didn't*!' She was vehement, but he almost laughed.

'It was just coincidence that they immediately called my bluff? If you didn't make up Lorraine's mind for her, who did?'

Jack Bastaple did. His letter to Caterine, that had made Lorraine afraid of losing Rolf. And Jenny couldn't tell Paul about that. Better let him believe Jenny had betrayed a confidence, a little thing, than tell him how Caterine had betrayed him.

She made a small helpless gesture, and Paul said, 'Don't let me detain you. I'm sure you and Ebby and Lorraine are wanting to plan the wedding.' He didn't sound angry, he sounded tired. He said, 'Although as a bridesmaid you'll probably outshine the bride.'

... As Caterine would have done, but I am Jenny. ... 'Paul—' she stretched a hand across the table to touch his hand. Last night he had drawn her into his arms; now he said:

'Run along,' as though she wearied him. And he was untouchable.

It was no use arguing or trying to explain, and she had a growing and desolate conviction that she might never get near to him again.

Timothy was still awake. She went into her room and he heard her and called, 'Auntie Jen?'

'What is it?'

She opened the communicating door and looked in on

him. He sounded pleased with himself, as though he had come up with a bright solution to a knotty problem.

'Auntie Jen, why don't you marry Father? Then you'll always stay here and he'll look after you.'

She heard her own voice, gay and teasing. 'Don't you think one wedding at a time's enough?'

Then she closed the door again, and sat on the side of her bed, face in her hands, knowing that she mustn't begin to cry.

CHAPTER NINE

Jenny stayed in her room that evening, and no one looked for her until Lorraine came back from the Perries'. Then, just after ten o'clock, Lorraine peeped in, all smiles.

Jenny had gone to bed with a magazine. She wasn't reading, but she certainly wouldn't be sleeping, so she was lying, propped up with an extra pillow, leafing through a glossy monthly.

Lorraine ran across to fling arms around her. 'Oh, Jenny, isn't it wonderful? I can't believe it, I just can't!' She did look quite radiant, and Jenny had to rejoice with her; she would have been a poor friend if she hadn't, although she was feeling sick at heart herself.

She said, 'I'm so glad. I do like Rolf, I know you're going to be happy.'

Oh yes!' Lorraine was confident of happiness. 'I thought this morning – why put off telling Paul till tomorrow, I'll feel the same tomorrow as I do now. So I drove over to the farm and I told Rolf, and Jenny, it wasn't so hard. You were right. Of course Paul isn't going to dismiss Rolf.'

'I'm glad,' said Jenny again. 'When are you getting married?'

Lorraine laughed softly, 'We thought Christmas Eve.' That didn't leave much time, but one way or another they had already had a long engagement.

'Paul didn't seem all that surprised,' Lorraine elaborated. 'Almost as though he'd expected it. He said he appreciated our telling him first.' She giggled slightly, mimicking her brother's deep voice: ' "I am the first to be told," he said, and I said, "Well – Jenny," and that didn't surprise him either. He said, "After Jenny, of course".'

She looked at Jenny fondly. 'You knew it would be all right, didn't you?'

'Yes.' For Lorraine and Rolf.

'There isn't anything the matter?' Jenny's pretence at gaiety must be slipping, because Lorraine sounded suddenly concerned, and Jenny explained:

'Paul thinks I did the persuading.'

Lorraine was indignant for a moment. 'He doesn't think I'm capable of making up my own mind?' Then she had to admit, 'It was the letter. I needed that. It wasn't Rolf, I'm sure, but one day it might have been, with some other girl, and like you said I had no right to complain.'

She grinned, 'I have now, though, and so has he, and I couldn't be more grateful to Caterine and whoever the man was.' Her grin faded. 'But we can't tell Paul that, can we?'

'Hardly,' said Jenny. It wasn't fair to spoil Lorraine's happiness tonight; she shrugged as though it didn't matter much and asked, 'What did Rolf's parents say?'

'They kept asking how Paul was taking it. His mother couldn't believe Rolf hadn't been thrown out of the house.'

She was joking, but Mrs. Perrie had needed reassuring, and she had kissed Lorraine, welcoming her as a daughter-in-law, with some defiance as though the vengeance of Tremain might strike at any moment.

'You will be my bridesmaid, won't you?' Lorraine asked, and Jenny said:

'I'd love to!'

There wasn't much risk of her outshining anyone. Lorraine would be a dazzling bride, and Jenny felt a hundred years old.

Next day the news was around. The phone was already ringing at breakfast time, friends offering congratulations, wanting to know when the wedding was. Lorraine was jumping up and down to answer the phone all through breakfast and Timmy was hard to get off to school, suspecting that he would be missing some excitement.

In the end Jenny had to run with him to catch the school bus. As they ran he panted, 'Don't forget John's coming to tea. Don't let Ebby forget she promised to make gingerbread men.'

'I'll remind her,' Jenny promised, and did as soon as she got back before she forgot herself.

Lorraine was spending the day with Rolf. They were buying the ring. Any one of the three rings that had fallen to Lorraine in the share-out of Caterine's jewellery was probably grander than the best Rolf could afford, but Lorraine wanted Rolf's ring, even if he did have to hobble into the shop to buy it for her. Lorraine anticipated a lovely day, but Jenny did not.

Jenny was right, Paul was at his most irascible. Mr. Morrison made no mention at all of the engagement and Paul was half-way through the morning mail when the phone on his desk rang and it was a reporter.

Yes, said Paul, he was delighted at his sister's choice. Lorraine and Rolf Perrie had been friends from childhood and no, he had not saved Rolf Perrie's life recently. That rescue operation had entailed a score or more men.

Paul didn't answer the phone again. Each time it rang Mr. Morrison took it, and when he said that Mr. Tremain was not in the office Jenny presumed that was because somebody wanted to discuss Miss Tremain and Mr. Perrie.

Maddeningly none of this seemed to impair Paul's efficiency. His dictation was crisper than ever, and when Jenny's pencil snapped he glared at her as though that was her fault too.

She had Mr. Morrison's sympathy. Once he almost winked at her. Perhaps it was hardly a wink, but his eyelids drooped in fellow-feeling when Paul asked if something was ready for signature and it wasn't.

It might have been if nothing had disturbed her, but she had brought them in coffee at eleven, and she had spoiled a couple of pages that had to be retyped. So it wasn't ready, and Paul snapped, 'I hope it will be when I get back. It has to go today,' and she shrilled:

'Well, of course it will. It isn't going to take me all day!'

'I'm glad to hear that,' he said.

She flopped in her chair when he went out of the

office and Mr. Morrison said, 'Don't take it personally.'

'It is personal.'

'No.' He shook his head at her. 'You know better than that. This marriage is not altogether to his liking, and you are drawing the fire because your mind is not altogether on your work.'

She typed another line, then she said, 'I never thought that Paul would do any of the things that Lorraine worried about, sacking Rolf, taking away the farm from his parents, telling her never to darken his doors again – all that melodrama. Did you?'

'It seemed unlikely,' Mr. Morrison conceded.

'I knew he wouldn't. I asked him and he said he wouldn't, but he thinks I told them what he said.'

'You didn't?'

'*No!*'

Mr. Morrison made his silent. 'Oh . . .'

'So this is personal.' Jenny smiled, but her lips were unsteady, and Mr. Morrison said quietly:

'Mr. Tremain almost invariably keeps his own counsel. If he feels that you betrayed a confidence I suggest you tell him, forcibly, that you did not.'

This time Jenny did smile. 'He isn't the easiest man to use force on.'

Mr. Morrison chuckled with her. Then he went back to his work and she went on with her typing. It was good advice. She wished she could follow it, but Paul wasn't going to listen to her, so what chance had she of telling him anything?

Moidores was full of activity that evening. Paul was not around, but Rolf was, and Lorraine had her engagement ring and plans for the wedding were going ahead. Half the population of Tremain seemed to be in the drawing-room, although in fact there was only Grace and Ben and four others, artists who were Lorraine's closest friends. Not Jack, for which Jenny was thankful.

Lorraine had gone down to the harbour earlier to ask them up and it was a little party with a lot of talk and laughter. Jenny joined in for a while, then went along to see how Timmy and his guest were faring. They were setting up and dismantling the train set, and arguing every inch of the way. Then she slipped out of the house for a breath of fresh air, and because she wanted to be alone.

She went across the springy turf of the cliff top gardens at the back of the house. The coastline and the sea spread out below her, and she neared the edge of the cliff where the gnarled old trees, planted a hundred years ago, made dark grotesque silhouettes against the skyline.

Paul stood by one of the trees, and when Jenny saw him he had already seen her and was turning, facing her. Her step quickened instinctively, she took a couple of paces almost running towards him, then she caught herself and steadied herself and went quietly.

He asked, 'What are you doing out here?'

'I came for some air. What are you?'

'I do sometimes walk in my garden. You're too near the cliff edge for night-time.'

The moon was out, she could see clearly and was as safe as he was. 'And it's cold,' he said. 'You'd better go in.'

He didn't want her staying, he didn't want her walking with him. She said, 'Lorraine's very happy and she could be penniless and Rolf would still love her.'

'Very romantic,' he said cynically, and she went on with what she was trying to tell him.

'And I told Lorraine all along that I didn't believe you'd sack Rolf, but I never told either of them that I'd asked you.'

'Just a coincidence?'

'Coincidences do happen.'

'Of course.' But there was irony in his voice. 'And now you'd better go back to the party, unless you want them all out here looking for you.'

He left her and walked away, along the cliff's edge overlooking the cove of Moidores. What could she do? How could she force him to believe her? She went back into the house, and gave a reasonable imitation of a girl without a care in the world.

Paul was in the office next morning and Jenny concentrated fervently on her work so that he could find no fault with that. The atmosphere was calm enough but hardly relaxing, and after lunch when she was alone with Mr. Morrison it was easier to type without making mistakes.

'Where is Paul?' she asked. It was easier without him, but empty.

'He's gone to St. Agnes,' said Mr. Morrison, 'to see the Frearsons.' Paul owned a crafts shop they ran, it sold 'Tremain' work, and Jenny frowned.

'But I thought that was tomorrow.' The appointment was down under Saturday morning.

'He changed it.' Mr. Morrison looked up at her. 'He's not in tomorrow. You didn't know that?'

'No.'

'You haven't straightened out that little matter?'

'I tried to. He wouldn't listen. He just walked away.'

'Going sailing. Leaving tonight, I believe.'

Without her, of course. Her eyes brimmed with sudden tears, and she looked down hastily and said brightly, 'He can always get away from it all for a while. He's lucky.'

'Not always,' said Mr. Morrison.

'I can't believe that.'

A few moments passed during which Mr. Morrison made a decision. He said, 'You once suggested that I did not like your sister.' Jenny remembered. 'I didn't dislike her,' Mr. Morrison insisted, 'but I didn't admire her.' Knowing what she knew now Jenny couldn't leap to Caterine's defence, and he went on:

'Now, Mr. Tremain is a man for whom I have a great respect and a great deal of affection.' The expressionless face softened briefly, then set in severe lines. 'I should be distressed to see him make a second mistake.'

He looked hard at Jenny and she faltered, 'A second mistake?' not sure if he was meaning her until he smiled.

'You,' he told her, 'have many attractive qualities, Miss Douglas. Certainly you have initiative.' She sat wondering what this was leading to. 'I hear that your trip on the *Mylor* was a success. Dan Blaskie expects you to be sailing with them again.'

'Not today,' she said ruefully, and Mr. Morrison who had sat with pen in hand during all this made a little squiggle of notes in the margin of the paper before him. As he wrote he said:

'A pity. Mr. Tremain could hardly walk away if he was at the wheel of a boat.'

On the *Mylor* she could have talked to Paul, or on the Witch's Rock. You saw things clearer out there, without interruptions or pretence. 'That's true,' she said.

'I should like you to take a message down to the Tremain Arms.' He could have phoned that, whatever it was.

'Yes?' Jenny waited.

'About the alterations in the saloon bar. Would you tell the Trevarricks that I'll be along this evening to discuss them?'

'Yes, I will. What about this?' She touched the typewriter.

'That can wait till Monday.'

'Thank you.' If she managed to get herself aboard the *Mylor* she could have the sack by Monday. She could be well and truly out of Moidores, or everything could be right again. It all depended. She was taking a gambler's risk, and at the door she looked back to say, 'Wish me luck.'

'With all my heart, Miss Douglas,' said Mr. Morrison.

Jenny changed her shoes and put on a thick coat, then rammed a few things into a large handbag and hurried. If Paul was already aboard she was a loser right away, he wasn't going to take her along if he knew about it.

But the *Mylor* dinghy was moored by the jetty, and she crossed her fingers and touched the studded black oak door of the Tremain Arms. She wouldn't have admitted being superstitious, but she needed all the luck she could get.

Mrs. Trevarrick took the message and smiled at Jenny, who had always seemed a nice girl to her, and from what they were saying could well be Mrs. Tremain before long.

It seemed romance was in the air. Miss Lorraine and Rolf Perrie coming together after all. Mrs. Trevarrick was a sentimental soul. She tried to get Jenny to stay, to have a drink, a cup of tea or coffee, and Jenny thanked her, said she would have loved to, but she was in a hurry; and Mrs. Trevarrick followed her out into the street still talking about what a nice young man Rolf Perrie was and what a lovely bride Miss Lorraine would make.

Dan Blaskie's pink-washed cottage was on the corner, the other side of the road from the Tremain Arms. Jenny knocked on the door with Mrs. Trevarrick still smiling at her.

Suppose Paul opened the door? He might have called for Dan. Then she could only ask, 'Will you take me with you?' and he would say, 'No.' Or she could be a coward and pretend she'd come to see Dan.

Dan answered. Maybe touching wood worked. He grinned at her and she asked, 'Are you going out to the *Mylor*?'

'No. Everything's ready, all ship-shape. Want to get aboard early, do ee?'

He was taking it for granted she was going. Luck *was* with her. 'Yes, please,' she said.

'Oright, m'dear.' He called back into the house to his wife, 'Back in no time,' and they walked together along the quayside and climbed into the dinghy.

It couldn't be this easy. Jenny was nervous as a cat on hot bricks, and not at all surprised when Dan asked what was troubling her.

He was bound to tell Paul that she had gone on ahead. She pleaded, 'Will you do something for me?'

'Name it.'

She twisted her hands together in her lap. 'Paul hasn't asked me to go sailing this time.'

That brought Dan's head up from between his shoulders, his leathery neck stretched like a tortoise coming out of its shell. 'Please don't tell him I'm on board,' she implored.

Dan faltered in his rowing. 'What's this, then? What's the skulking for?'

'He hasn't said I can't go. You could say you took it for granted I'd got permission. Well, you did, didn't you?'

He growled, 'Sure of it I was,' looking at Jenny beneath beetling brows as if she had taken advantage of him. The dinghy was making no progress now, while Dan considered whether to go on or back. He demanded, 'Why didn't you ask him, then?'

'He wasn't in a good mood this morning.'

'Reckon he'll be better tempered out there?'

'He usually is, isn't he?'

'Aye, as a rule.'

'So please don't say anything.'

Dan brooded for a while longer, then he dipped the oars once more, and the dinghy skimmed on towards the *Mylor*. 'Not unless I'm asked.' He yielded that much, and she accepted it gratefully.

It would give her a chance. Someone who had seen her being rowed across the bay might tell Paul, and then he would certainly ask Dan. But there was a chance of her getting out to sea before she was discovered. Paul might let her stay aboard if he found her in harbour, but she would rather stay hidden until they had passed the point where he hadn't much option.

She would admit she had hoodwinked Dan, she would see that no blame attached to him.

Dan wasted no time. He rowed off as soon as she scrambled aboard, and she went at once through the forward two-door hatch into the small room with the sails and stores lockers, down the steps into the cabin where she had slept last Saturday.

The bed was not made up. She found blankets and sheets in the tin trunk, and three foam mattresses, one of which she presumed was hers, in a cupboard under the settee in the main cabin.

It was cold. No lamps or stoves were lit, and Dan's last words had been a warning that she could be in for a longish wait. 'I'll wait,' she'd said. She had to, now. She made up her bed, and then went back through the access doors past the foot of the mainmast and into the main cabin again.

She was apprehensive, but she was glad to be here. It would have been unbearable tonight, in her own quiet room in Moidores, knowing that Paul had left her behind. Mr. Morrison would cover for her with Ebby and Timmy, and Paul too until Paul left. Then he would explain where she had gone.

That had been a surprising thing he had done. Putting this idea into her head, and putting himself in a very awkward position when the *Mylor* sailed back into Tremain.

She couldn't even light a lamp, although it was almost bound to be dark before they left harbour. She watched Tremain through the porthole, seeing the lights come on, trying to distinguish tiny figures on the quayside, and when dusk fell rain came, spattering on the porthole. The chill was beginning to reach her bones and she went to her own cabin and got into bed, fully dressed except for shoes, and huddled under the blankets.

She could see nothing through the porthole. There were no stars or moon tonight to silver the sea. She could hear the wind and the slapping water and it sounded like a bleak night, so that she wondered if Paul might change his mind.

She would look a right idiot if he did, and she was stuck out here until Dan rowed over for her in the morning. She giggled weakly at the thought. She was warm under the blankets now, lulled by the movement and creakings of the boat, and Paul would come, she knew he would. She closed her eyes, remembering the blissful sanctuary of his arms around her.

The sound of engines woke her. *Mylor* was leaving harbour and she stayed where she was, curled snug and quiet in her bunk.

There was no sound of footsteps on deck. Dan was probably in the main cabin, but she daren't even go along there until they were well out to sea. The wheelhouse was directly overhead and Paul would overhear voices.

She was a stowaway and he was likely to blow his top when he saw her, but she could take that, although now that the prospect was near she had butterflies in her stomach and an uncomfortable tightening in her throat. He couldn't throw her overboard, but he could make her feel like jumping.

It was too late to change her mind now, unless she stayed a stowaway and starved till Sunday.

She looked for the Witch's Rock, but rain masked the porthole. It wouldn't be pleasant up there in the wheel-house, although it would be cosy in the cabin. Dan would probably come looking for her. He'd have to, for his own alibi. He'd brought her aboard, and he'd have to say something about that before long, or Paul would know he had an uneasy conscience.

But Dan didn't come. The engines were quiet now. They were well out of harbour and the *Mylor* was powered by sail.

Jenny stayed where she was for an hour or more, then she crept very quietly through to the main cabin. It was a choppy set, the boat was pitching, she had to take care, and there were no lamps on in here either, nor was the stove lit.

No sign of life at all, so both men must be up on deck. She went to her cabin to get the waterproof coat from one of the lockers that Dan had found for her last time. Then she went up on deck herself.

She was prepared for rain, but it was teeming down and seemed dark as pitch around. The decks looked slippery and hazardous, and she held on to the rail, looking back at the wheelhouse. As she stood in a patch of light she heard Paul roar over the sound of wind and slapping sails, 'Get below!'

Well, he'd seen her. He knew she was here. Perhaps Dan had already told him. The reckoning was to come, but he might be less annoyed if she made herself useful.

She lit the lamps, thankful that she had followed Dan around last time, learning all she could. Then she lit the calor gas stove, and looked for food. The galley was well stocked and there were a couple of flasks. Coffee and soup, when she unscrewed and checked them.

The cabin was warm in no time, and Jenny alternated between guilt and high delight. She had gatecrashed, but that wasn't so dreadful. There was room, she was doing no harm. She was so enchanted with the *Mylor* that she couldn't keep her fingers from stroking the wooden panelling on the walls, moving the cushions around, poking around the store cupboard.

The ship moved and breathed like a living thing, and Jenny told it, 'You are so beautiful,' and although she laughed at herself the words didn't sound ridiculous.

Then she put on her waterproof again, and went up the companionway into the wheelhouse. Paul was in glistening black oilskins, large and looming and dripping wet.

'Where did you come from?' he demanded.

'You wouldn't believe I swam out?' But he was probably in no mood for jokes and she admitted, 'Dan brought me, but he thought you'd said I could come.'

'Why didn't you ask me?'

'You might have said no, and I wanted to talk to you, and you can't walk away from the wheel, can you?'

'Not on a night like this in a shipping lane.'

'Where's Dan?'

'At home.'

So he had intended to make this trip alone and he would have said no and she was an intruder. She should have said, 'Sorry,' but she wasn't sorry. She asked, 'Where are we going?'

'We should be going back to Tremain.'

'No!' she wailed, then as the deck sloped she slithered, and Paul grabbed her and ordered:

'Get below, for God's sake, you'll be overboard!' He shoved her towards the companionway and she climbed down a few steps so that she was sheltered but could still look up at him.

'Please don't turn back,' she pleaded. '*Please.* I'll be no trouble, I promise. I'll stay in my own cabin. It's a big boat.'

'Not that big.'

'This is ridiculous!' she shrilled desperately. 'Going all the way back just to get rid of me. What am I supposed to be, a jinx aboard? Do you think I whistled up the storm?'

He laughed suddenly, 'I wouldn't put it past you,' and she laughed too, because he wasn't angry, he wasn't turning back, he was glad she was here.

'Then you'd better maroon me on Witch's Rock with the sea-witch.'

'No,' he said. 'Oh no.'

The rain and spray blew in gusts so that in spite of the protective shield of hatch-coaming it was wet and cold in the wheelhouse. She wanted him in, out of the storm. 'I've lit the lamps,' she said. 'And the food's ready any time. How long before we can anchor?'

'Another hour before we reach harbour.'

'Not Tremain?'

'No.'

'I'll bring the coffee up.'

She brought the flask and half filled the brown enamel mugs, but even so they slopped over with the rise and fall of the boat. This time she was prepared and kept her footing, and stayed beside him under the awning and drank some of her coffee.

Then she said, 'I came to tell you again that I didn't tell Lorraine what you said. Rolf was prepared to lose his job and Lorraine was ready to go with him anywhere.'

'I'm glad to hear that.'

'You believe me?'

'Yes.'

A hooter signalled mournfully as the lights of a passing ship showed in the distance. Paul answered with the *Mylor*'s siren and the echoes seemed to linger. It was a larger ship than this, probably carrying cargo. Jenny watched it pass and vanish into the darkness, then she said, 'I think they'll be happy.'

'I hope so.'

He was cynical because he thought Caterine had married him for his money, and perhaps she had, but she had made sacrifices too. She had given as well as taken. Jenny said, 'Maybe Caterine did enjoy being the wife of a rich man, but she gave up her career for you.'

He sounded amused. 'Not for me. That was her choice.'

'But—' Jenny gulped and was silent. Caterine had always said it was Paul who insisted she gave up acting. 'Paul won't hear of me acting again,' Jenny remembered her telling them before she married, and since, lots of times since.

'But,' Jenny faltered, 'the work she was offered you made her turn down. Didn't you?'

'Acting's an overcrowded profession.' He was watching the compass as he spoke. 'Can you see someone who wasn't an established name getting genuine offers years after they'd left the business?'

'She didn't?'

'She had theatrical friends. There was talk about productions, but anyone who suggested Caterine for a role knew there was no risk of the offer being taken up. She never considered going back to work.'

'You didn't stop her?'

'Why should I?'

'But I thought that – Caterine *told* me, she told everyone you wouldn't let her.'

'That was one of Caterine's fantasies.'

Hadn't Grace said that Caterine enjoyed saying, 'Paul wouldn't let me.' Jenny had often thought that herself, although she had believed that Caterine had sacrificed her career for love. Caterine had had talent and promise, but it was no real surprise to hear that she had preferred the pampered life. Acting was chancy and hard work, Queen Caterina of Tremain was a cushier role.

That left one thing unexplained. Jenny said suddenly, 'But – the quarrel?'

'What quarrel?' Hands on the wheel, he turned to look at her, and she blurted:

'The night Caterine died, she'd asked you, hadn't she if she could go back to the stage, and you'd said no? Wasn't that why she suddenly decided to visit me? She was upset, crying. Wasn't she?'

He said heavily, 'Who told you this?'

'Lorraine. She was there.'

'She was not there.'

But Lorraine had told her why Caterine was weeping,

why she had driven that car erratically and too fast.

Paul said, 'Lorraine may have heard Caterine's version, but take my word there were no witnesses to that scene.'

Then what was Paul's version? Jenny whispered, 'What happened?'

He said wryly, 'Nothing that matters now. Nothing that really mattered then. My wife was welcome to a career, but not to a lover.'

'You *knew*?' Did he know who? How did he know? 'How?'

'More to the point – how did you?'

'There was part of a letter. Lorraine and I found it while we were clearing the cupboards. That was what made up Lorraine's mind. She thought at first it might be Rolf and she was jealous, and she knew then how much Rolf meant to her.' She added quickly, 'It wasn't Rolf.'

'No,' said Paul. He knew who it was. 'Why didn't you tell me this?'

'I didn't want you hurt, I didn't think you knew. I don't think it was really anything, just a flirtation.'

'Thank you,' he said dryly, 'no one ever tried to protect me before. I know what it was and I suspect you do. Caterine was a good actress, if I hadn't been sure of my facts I might have believed her.'

Jenny could imagine Caterine protesting her innocence, claiming that she was wounded to the heart, that she was going to her sister's ... getting away from Paul because she was guilty and afraid.

She would never have considered that she might lose Paul Tremain and the rich life, for a stupid little infidelity that didn't really count. She had kept her head when she met Lorraine, with tears still on her face, and sobbed out the old story, Paul wouldn't let her go back to acting, only this time, for the first time, there had been this horrible quarrel.

Lorraine wouldn't ask Paul about that. No one would dare to ask Paul, and Caterine would get to Jenny's and it would all blow over, because it wasn't really true that she had been unfaithful. Jack Bastaple didn't count, Jack

Bastaple was nothing. . . .

The things that counted for Caterine were the things that Paul Tremain could give her. Her jewellery in the bank vault and in the wall safe. Oh, she would have planned on coming back, poor silly Caterine, running scared for the first time in her life.

Jenny said huskily, 'She paid.'

'Too high a price,' said Paul. 'I should never have let her drive that car.'

'Would you have taken her back?'

'Probably.'

There were a few lights a long way away, little clusters interspersed by darkness. They were heading for a lonely coastline.

Paul said, 'When I first saw Caterine it was like a blow between the eyes. I seemed to recognize her. I'd never seen her before, I'd never even seen a photograph of her, but I felt that she was part of me, that she'd shared everything that had ever happened to me.

'It sounds insane.' He looked at Jenny and she said:

'Go on.'

'I knew her,' he said, 'but she wasn't the woman I knew. I stopped looking for that woman in her a long time ago, but she was beautiful and talented and she amused me. Even her greed was tolerable, it was so obvious.

'Yes, I'd have taken her back. I had an affection for her that I thought was as deep as love would go for me.'

But he was in no way a shallow man. He was deep as the sea and enduring as the rocks. In his arms she could live for ever.

Her lips tasted salt with spray and she went closer to him. He put an arm around her and they stood at the wheel of the *Mylor* and he said quietly, 'My ancestors have been here for a thousand years. Do you believe there's such a thing as a race memory?'

They said so, those who should know. That we remembered sometimes, fleetingly, things that had happened to the men and women from whom we came. An echo from the past, a whisper in the blood.

186

She said, 'In the Witch's Cave?'

'What I thought I saw in Caterine,' said Paul, 'was you.'

'Was there a sea witch?'

'There's no record. It's just one of the old Cornish legends.'

'If there was,' said Jenny, 'I think she came back.'

'She has,' said Paul. He kissed her slow and hard, and there were no lights on the cliffs ahead as the sails folded and the engines purred and the *Mylor* came to a quiet harbourage.

FREE!

*Harlequin
Romance
Catalogue*

Here is a wonderful opportunity to read many of the Harlequin Romances you may have missed.

The HARLEQUIN ROMANCE CATALOGUE lists hundreds of titles which possibly are no longer available at your local bookseller. To receive your copy, just fill out the coupon below, mail it to us, and we'll rush your catalogue to you!

Following this page you'll find a sampling of a few of the Harlequin Romances listed in the catalogue. Should you wish to order any of these immediately, kindly check the titles desired and mail with coupon.

To: **HARLEQUIN READER SERVICE, Dept. N 310**
M.P.O. Box 707, Niagara Falls, N.Y. 14302
Canadian address: Stratford, Ont., Canada

☐ Please send me the free Harlequin Romance Catalogue.

☐ Please send me the titles checked.

I enclose $＿＿＿＿＿ (No C.O.D.'s), All books are 60c each. To help defray postage and handling cost, please add 25c.

Name ＿＿＿＿＿＿＿＿＿＿＿＿＿＿＿＿＿＿＿＿＿＿＿

Address ＿＿＿＿＿＿＿＿＿＿＿＿＿＿＿＿＿＿＿＿＿

City/Town ＿＿＿＿＿＿＿＿＿＿＿＿＿＿＿＿＿＿＿

State/Prov. ＿＿＿＿＿＿＿＿＿＿＿ Zip＿＿＿＿

Have You Missed Any of These
Harlequin Romances?

- ☐ 412 NURSE TRENTON
  Caroline Trench
- ☐ 416 DOCTOR LUCY   Barbara Allen
- ☐ 422 THEN COME KISS ME
  Mary Burchell
- ☐ 434 DEAR DOCTOR EVERETT
  Jean S. Macleod
- ☐ 446 TO PLEASE THE DOCTOR
  Marjorie Moore
- ☐ 454 NURSE IN LOVE   Jane Arbor
- ☐ 482 NURSE HARLOWE   Jane Arbor
- ☐ 908 ELIZABETH BROWNE,
  CHILDREN'S NURSE
  Rosalind Brett
- ☐ 909 DESERT DOORWAY
  Pamela Kent
- ☐ 919 DEAR INTRUDER   Jane Arbor
- ☐ 922 THE TAMING OF NURSE
  CONWAY   Nora Sanderson
- ☐ 931 CHARGE NURSE   Hilary Neal
- ☐ 934 MY DEAR COUSIN
  Celine Conway
- ☐ 937 THE CASE FOR NURSE
  SHERIDAN   Nora Sanderson
- ☐ 943 ENEMY LOVER
  Pamela Kent
- ☐ 975 SISTER OF THE
  HOUSEMASTER
  Eleanor Farnes
- ☐ 979 DOCTOR OVERBOARD
  Catherine Airlie
- ☐ 1107 THEY MET IN ZANZIBAR
  Kathryn Blair
- ☐ 1120 HEART IN HAND
  Margaret Malcolm
- ☐ 1122 WHISTLE AND I'LL COME
  Flora Kidd
- ☐ 1124 THE NEW ZEALANDER
  Joyce Dingwell
- ☐ 1145 YOUNG DOCTOR YERDLEY
  Anne Durham
- ☐ 1150 THE BRIDE OF MINGALAY
  Jean S. Macleod
- ☐ 1180 ROSE OF THE DESERT
  Roumelia Lane
- ☐ 1209 THE STUBBORN DR. STEPHEN
  Elizabeth Houghton
- ☐ 1212 HIDEAWAY HEART
  Roumelia Lane

- ☐ 1214 THE MARSHALL FAMILY
  Mary Burchell
- ☐ 1220 ISLE OF THE HUMMING-
  BIRD   Juliet Armstrong
- ☐ 1242 NEW DOCTOR AT NORTHMOOR
  Anne Durham
- ☐ 1254 THE MASTER OF KEILLS
  Jean S. Macleod
- ☐ 1257 DOCTOR AT VILLA RONDA
  Iris Danbury
- ☐ 1289 THE MUCH-LOVED NURSE
  Pauline Ash
- ☐ 1297 DENTAL NURSE AT DENLEY'S
  Marjorie Lewty
- ☐ 1306 A HANDFUL OF SILVER
  Isobel Chace
- ☐ 1310 TAWNY ARE THE LEAVES
  Wynne May
- ☐ 1316 CAN THIS BE LOVE
  Margaret Malcolm
- ☐ 1321 BUSH HOSPITAL
  Gladys Fullbrook
- ☐ 1323 MOONLIGHT ON THE WATER
  Hilda Nickson
- ☐ 1325 NO SOONER LOVED
  Pauline Garnar
- ☐ 1327 MORE THAN GOLD
  Hilda Pressley
- ☐ 1329 NURSE LISTER'S MILLSTONE
  Marjorie Norrell
- ☐ 1332 DON'T WALK ALONE
  Jane Donnelly
- ☐ 1333 KEEPER OF THE HEART
  Gwen Westwood
- ☐ 1336 THE CYPRESS GARDEN
  Jane Arbor
- ☐ 1344 THE DANGEROUS DELIGHT
  Violet Winspear
- ☐ 1349 ETERNAL SUMMER
  Anne Hampson
- ☐ 1379 A TOUCH OF STARLIGHT
  Rosemary Pollock
- ☐ 1380 RELUCTANT MASQUERADE
  Henrietta Reid
- ☐ 1388 UNWARY HEART
  Anne Hampson
- ☐ 1397 IF LOVE WERE WISE
  Elizabeth Hoy

All books are 60c. Please use the handy order coupon.

DD

Have You Missed Any of These
Harlequin Romances?

☐ 449 NURSE IN TRAINING
Elizabeth Hoy
☐ 476 NURSE JESS
Joyce Dingwell
☐ 906 NURSE MOLLY
Marjorie Norrell
☐ 932 NURSE'S DILEMMA
Hilda Pressley
☐ 941 MAYENGA FARM
Kathryn Blair
☐ 948 ISLANDS OF SUMMER
Anne Weale
☐ 950 KINGFISHER TIDE
Jane Arbor
☐ 952 A COTTAGE IN SPAIN
Rosalind Brett
☐ 954 DOCTOR WESTLAND
Kathryn Blair
☐ 956 TAKE ME WITH YOU
Mary Burchell
☐ 958 YOUNG BAR   Jane Fraser
☐ 960 MAN OF DESTINY
Rose Burghley
☐ 962 NURSE MADELINE OF EDEN
GROVE   Marjorie Norrell
☐ 964 PROJECT SWEETHEART
Joyce Dingwell
☐ 969 NURSE AFLOAT   Jane Marnay
☐ 971 NURSE RIVERS' SECRET
Anne Durham
☐ 987 SENIOR STAFF NURSE
Hilda Pressley
☐ 994 JUBILEE HOSPITAL
Jan Tempest
☐ 1001 NO PLACE FOR SURGEONS
Elizabeth Gilzean
☐ 1004 THE PATH OF THE MOONFISH
Betty Beaty
☐ 1006 THE COURAGEOUS HEART
Jane Marnay
☐ 1010 DOCTOR OF RESEARCH
Elizabeth Houghton
☐ 1015 SWEET ARE THE WAYS
Essie Summers
☐ 1018 HOSPITAL IN THE TROPICS
Gladys Fullbrook
☐ 1020 NO JUST CAUSE
Susan Barrie

☐ 1023 THE SWEET SURRENDER
Rose Burghley
☐ 1030 THE BLACK BENEDICTS
Anita Charles
☐ 1034 NURSE MEG'S DECISION
Hilary Neal
☐ 1042 PROMISE THE DOCTOR
Marjorie Norrell
☐ 1048 HIGH MASTER OF CLERE
Jane Arbor
☐ 1050 NURSE ADELE
Hilda Nickson
☐ 1076 BELLS IN THE WIND
Kate Starr
☐ 1087 A HOME FOR JOCELYN
Eleanor Farnes
☐ 1108 SUMMER EVERY DAY
Jane Arbor
☐ 1115 THE ROMANTIC HEART
Norrey Ford
☐ 1131 THE BOLAMBO AFFAIR
Rosalind Brett
☐ 1142 SECRET HEIRESS
Eleanor Farnes
☐ 1152 A GARLAND OF MARIGOLDS
Isobel Chace
☐ 1210 A FRIEND OF THE FAMILY
Hilda Nickson
☐ 1230 CROWN OF CONTENT
Janice Gray
☐ 1241 NURSE BARLOW'S JINX
Marjorie Norrell
☐ 1277 STRANGER'S TRESPASS
Jane Arbor
☐ 1292 FALCON'S KEEP
Henrietta Reid
☐ 1309 THE HILLS OF MAKETU
Gloria Bevan
☐ 1341 FIRE IS FOR SHARING
Doris E. Smith
☐ 1354 WHEN LOVE'S BEGINNING
Mary Burchell
☐ 1366 DESIGN FOR LOVING
Margaret Baumann
☐ 1371 DANCING ON MY HEART
Belinda Dell
☐ 1377 SISTER DARLING
Marjorie Norrell

All books are 60c. Please use the handy order coupon.

FF

Golden Harlequin Library

A Treasury of Harlequin Romances!

Many of the all time favorite Harlequin Romance Novels have not been available, until now, since the original printing. But on this special introductory offer, they are yours in an exquisitely bound, rich gold hardcover with royal blue imprint. Three complete unabridged novels in each volume. And the cost is so very low you'll be amazed!

Handsome, Hardcover Library Editions at Paperback Prices! ONLY $1.95 each volume.

This very special collection of classic Harlequin Romances would be a distinctive addition to your library. And imagine what a delightful gift they'd make for any Harlequin reader!

Start your collection now. See reverse of this page for **SPECIAL INTRODUCTORY OFFER!**